THE BESTSELLER

By Stephen Leather

Would you kill to write a bestseller? Well Adrian Slater says that he's prepared to do just that – and announces the fact in a creative writing class. Lecturer Dudley Grose is convinced that Slater is a psychopath and means what he says. But the Dean of the university doesn't believe him and neither do the cops. But when a student on the course vanishes and her bathroom is awash with blood, the police wonder if Slater has actually carried out his threat, and if the book he's writing contains the evidence that will put him away.

CHAPTER 1

MARINA DEL RAY, CALIFORNIA. ONE YEAR AGO.

Lightning flashed and Kirsty flinched and she jumped again two seconds later when a crack of thunder split the Californian night sky to her left. It had started to rain the moment she'd walked into the marina, small spots at first but the moment that she'd set foot on the wooden pier that led to the yachts it had started to come down in sheets and now she was soaked to the skin. She wiped her face with her hand. Part of her, the sensible part, knew that she should just turn around and go home. But the other part, the part that kept her awake at night, was forcing her to go on, She had to know for sure. She had to know the truth.

The main pier jutted out into the center of the marina and smaller piers branched off it, left and right. The wooden planks creaked as she headed towards Wilson's yacht. Kirsty had been there three times before, once to go sailing with Wilson, the second time for lunch and the third time.... She shuddered. She didn't want to think about what had happened the third time.

Something small and furry ran across her path and she stifled a scream. She stopped and took slow deep breaths as she tried to quiet her racing heart. She didn't want to be at the marina, she wanted to be at home in bed, either asleep or watching TV or reading a book, but she had to be there. There was no going back, she had to know if she was going crazy or if Eddie Wilson really wanted to kill her.

Lightning flashed again and this time she was ready for the crack of thunder that came a few seconds later. Wilson's yacht was called THE WRITE WAY; it was just over thirty feet long with a single mast, the sail rolled up and hidden within a blue nylon sock. The yacht was in darkness. Wilson was the only owner who lived on his boat, all the rest were toys for weekend sailors. About half were yachts and catamarans but the rest were motorboats, floating gin palaces that rarely travelled more than a few miles or so from the marina.

The rain got heavier as she walked along the wooden pier towards the yacht. She stopped when she reached the stern and looked around. The marina was deserted and there had been no one in the office at the entrance. The metal mesh gate that led to the boats was never locked. She took her cell phone from her bag and covered it with her left hand to protect it from the rain as she peered at the screen. No one had called and there were no text messages. She'd arranged to meet Wilson for dinner at a Mexican restaurant that he'd said was one of his favorites, so hopefully he'd be sitting at the bar sipping a margarita while she did what she had to do. She switched off the phone and put it back in her pocket.

The yacht was tethered to the pier with ropes at either end and a third in the middle, and there was a power cable and a water hose snaking from a box by the stern into the rear cabin. She stepped carefully off the pier and onto the deck, holding on to the cabin roof to keep her balance as the boat shifted under her weight. Her heart was racing and she took slow, deep breaths to calm herself down. "It's okay," she muttered. "We go in, we look at his laptop and we get out. Easy peasy lemon squeazy."

She reached into the bag and pulled out bolt-cutters that she'd bought from a hardware store that morning along with two padlocks so that she could practice cutting the shackles. It took her only seconds to remove the lock and she tossed it into the water before pushing the hatch open. The wood grated and rain splattered inside. She ducked down into the cabin just as another bolt of lightning flashed out over the sea. It was harder to close the hatch than it had been to open it and she had to use all her weight to force it shut.

She stood in the darkness, listening to the sound of her own breathing. The boat was rocking from side to side in the wind and the metal lines rattled against the mast. She swallowed but her mouth was so dry that she almost gagged. She reached into her bag and pulled out a flashlight. She'd put duct tape across the glass with a small hole cut into it so that the light would be focused into a thin, tight beam. It was a trick she'd read in a thriller once, and she grinned to herself when she switched it on and discovered that it worked. The thin beam illuminated a section of the wall not much bigger than a dinner plate and even someone walking along the pier wouldn't be able to see the light.

At the far end of the main cabin was a door that led through to the sleeping area. There was a double bed there, she knew. With dark red silk sheets, the color of dried blood. That was where she'd gone on the third visit to the boat. She shuddered. Water plopped from her wet hair onto the floor and she wiped her face with her sleeve as she played the beam of light along the wall and down to the built-in desk, being careful to avoid the brass porthole even though it was the side of the yacht facing away from the pier. Wilson's MacBook Pro was there, open but switched off. There was a wooden chair in front of the desk and she sat down and pressed the button to turn on the computer. As the screen lit up she switched off the flashlight and placed it on the desk. There were three drawers on the right hand side of the desk and she pulled open the top one as she waited for the Mac to boot up.

There was a sketch pad in the drawer and she took it out. She flicked open the pad and her eyes widened when she saw the drawing on the first page. It was a caricature, a wide-eyed blonde with a pony tail sitting at an old-fashioned typewriter and above her head was a thought bubble filled with cuddly toys. The blonde had large breasts straining at the material of her too-tight shirt and Kirsty self-consciously put her hand to her chest. She'd seen

Wilson with the sketchpad during class but had always assumed that he was taking notes. "Bastard," she whispered.

The laptop finished booting up and she leaned forward and checked the icons on the desktop. There was only one Word document and it was titled 'The Bestseller'. Kirsty shook her head in disgust. She'd always thought that he was joking when he'd said that was the title of his book.

She clicked on the file and it opened. She read the opening paragraphs with a growing look of disgust on her face. "Bastard, bastard, bastard," she muttered. She stood up, switched on the flashlight and went through the galley and pushed open the door to the bedroom. There were cupboards above the bed and she pulled them open. There were two spare pillows inside and she took them out and tossed them onto the bed. There was a large book against the side of the cupboard and next to it a bulky leather roll. She took out the book and opened it. It was a medical book. Anatomy. There were yellow Post-its marking several of the pages, all concerned with the joints. Knees, elbows, hips, the neck. She threw the book down and took out the roll. She knew from its weight what it contained. Her heart was pounding as she sat down on the bed and put the roll in her lap, holding the flashlight between her teeth as she used both hands to untie the two leather straps that secured the bundle. She opened it out to reveal a dozen gleaming steel knives with black wooden handles.

"You evil bastard," she muttered as she stared down at the knives. She knew now that everything that Wilson had written in his book was true. He was planning to kill her and dismember her body, hiding the pieces God knows where. She heard a peal of thunder, closer this time.

She retied the bundle and stood up. The knives weren't proof but what Wilson had written on his laptop most definitely was. It was as good as a confession. She had to get a copy and take it to the police. Then they'd stop him. She patted the back pocket of her jeans to reassure herself that the thumbdrive was there, then opened the door and stepped into the main cabin, the tight beam of her flashlight playing across the floor. She yelped when the beam found a pair of black cowboy boots.

"Surprise!" It was Wilson. His voice was a soft whisper, barely audible over the noise of the wind and the pattering of raindrops against the hull.

The flashlight fell from Kirsty's hands, hit the floor, and rolled against the wall. She bent down, her heart racing and grabbed it, thanking God silently because the bulb hadn't broken. She tucked the bundle of knives under her right arm and held the flashlight with both hands as she played the thin beam around the cabin.

Wilson had gone. For a brief moment she wondered if she'd imagined him and then there was a flash of lightning and she saw him standing with his back to the bulkhead by the desk. His jet black hair was wet from the rain and he had a five o'clock shadow. Water was dripping down his face and he was grinning. Then just as quickly the cabin was plunged into darkness and she searched for him with the beam as a roll of thunder made her stomach vibrate.

He was standing by the computer, his hand resting on the keyboard. "You peeked," he said. She played the beam of light over his face. His clothes were soaked through but he was grinning. It was a cruel grin, almost savage. He was tall and wiry, and dressed all in black: shirt, jeans, cowboy boots, and a long coat from which water was plopping onto the floor.

Kirsty tried to speak but the words caught in her throat. "I, I, I…"

"Yes, I know," said Wilson. He took a step towards her, still smiling.

She held up the bundle of knives. "I know what you were planning to do," she said.

"What? What exactly do you think I was planning to do, Kirsty?"

"You know."

"Tell me. Maybe it's all been a terrible misunderstanding."

Lightning flashed and it was followed immediately by a crack of thunder. The storm was right overhead. The boat was rocking from side to side and Kirsty was having trouble maintaining her balance. She held up the roll of knives. "You're mad," she said.

He smiled easily. "I'm a little unhappy at the way you broke in here, but I wouldn't say I'm mad."

"You know what I mean," she said. "Deranged, Insane."

"Oh come on, Kirsty. You need to relax. Come on. Big breaths."

Kirsty gestured at the laptop with the bundle. "You were going to do it, weren't you? You were going to kill me and write about me."

"It's a novel, Kirsty."

"You were going to do it! For real!"

"It's a work of fiction."

"I read it," said Kirsty. "I read what you wrote. You're going to kill me. Then you're going to butcher me." She held up the bundle and waved it at him. "With these! You bastard, you had it all planned. You were going to kill me and write a sick book about it."

Wilson shook his head sadly. Kirsty realized that he had shifted his body so that she couldn't see his right hand. She moved the beam but as she did he stepped forward. He was holding a frying pan and he swung it at her, hard. She jumped back but he was too quick and the pan slammed into the bundle of knives and sent it hurtling from her hand. The bundle burst apart as it hit the wall behind her and the knives spilled out and crashed to the floor.

Wilson swished the pan from side to side. Lightning flashed again. Kirsty braced herself for the crack of thunder but it never came.

Kirsty stepped back, her shoe crunching on one of the knives. "It's going to be all right, Kirsty," said Wilson.

He moved to the side, out of the beam of the flashlight, and Kirsty's heart pounded as she tried to keep the light on him. "Not scared of the dark, are you, Kirsty?" said Wilson.

Kirsty bent down, grabbed one of the knives with her left hand and straightened up, holding it out in front of her. "Don't come near me," she said.

"Now that just looks awkward," said Wilson. "You're not a leftie. You'd be so much better off with the knife in your right."

"Stop talking to me," said Kirsty. She waved the knife from side to side. He was right. It felt wrong in her left hand.

He took a step towards her and she shuffled back, her left heel scraping against another knife.

"You should swap them around," said Wilson. "Have the knife in your right hand, the flashlight in your left. Trust me, you'll do more damage if I try to do this." He lunged forward, making a grab for her left hand but she jerked away and lashed out with the knife. He jumped back, grinning. "See, if you'd had the knife in your right hand you'd have got me then."

"I just want to go home," said Kirsty, her voice trembling.

"But you've only just got here, sweetheart," said Wilson. He jerked a thumb towards the bedroom. "How about a quickie, just for old time's sake."

"Please, just let me go home."

"Sweetheart, will you take a look at yourself. You're the one with the knife. You're the one who broke in. Who's the one being threatened here?" He stepped to the left, out of the beam of the flashlight, and Kirsty swung it around to keep the light on him.

He lashed out with the pan and it smacked against the knife. Kirsty cried out in pain as it went spinning across the cabin.

Lightning flashed and as it did she saw him with the pan raised high. As the cabin went dark again he brought the pan crashing down on the flashlight. The impact almost wrenched her arm from its socket but she managed to keep hold of the flashlight as the glass smashed and the light went out. She threw the broken flashlight towards where she thought Wilson was standing but when it hit the wall of the cabin she knew that she had missed.

She dropped down onto her hands and knees and groped around in the dark, trying to find one of the knives.

Lightning flashed and she saw Wilson standing in front of her, a manic grin on his face. The pan had gone and in its place was a bread knife with a serrated edge. Just as Kirsty screamed, the cabin was plunged into darkness again. She scuttled backwards on all fours, her breath coming in ragged gasps.

"Kirsty, it's all right," whispered Wilson. "Just go with the flow. It'll soon be over."

She sat back on her heels and held up her hands. She was shaking uncontrollably. Something flashed across her right palm and then she felt the pain and realized that he'd slashed her with the knife. She shuffled backwards, hyperventilating.

"Don't fight it, sweetheart," he said. "It'll be so much easier if you just let it happen."

Kirsty could feel blood trickling down her palms and the cut flesh was stinging so hard that her eyes were watering.

Lighting flashed again and she saw Wilson crouched in front of her, an evil grin on his face. He lashed out with the knife and Kirsty threw up her hands just as the cabin was plunged into darkness. The blade slashed across the fingers of her left hand. Again there was just a stinging sensation and she bit down on her lower lip, fighting the urge to scream.

Wilson laughed manically and she felt the knife bite into her left shoulder, ripping through her shirt and slicing through the skin. This time she screamed and flailed out her hands. Her left hand touched something and she grabbed for it. It was the blade of the knife, she realized, and as her fingers tightened on it Wilson pulled the knife back and the serrated blade tore through her hand.

She fell back, screaming, then rolled onto her front and began to crawl away from him on her hands and knees. Her fingers scrabbled over the wooden floor and she gasped as she felt the handle of a knife brush against the little finger of her right hand. She grabbed it and gently reached out with her left hand to touch the blade. It was about six inches long. The blade felt wet and she shivered as she realized it was because it was covered in blood from the cuts on her hands.

"Ready or not, here I come," whispered Wilson in the darkness.

Kirsty held her breath and turned her head slowly from side to side, listening intently. She heard a slight scraping sound, his shoe scraping across the deck, maybe. And she could hear him breathing, slowly and evenly. She turned the knife around in her hand so that she was grasping the handle in her fist, the blade pointing down. She kicked off both her shoes.

She heard another scrape. He was moving towards her. She sat back on her heels and held her left hand out, fingers splayed, still holding her breath. Then lightning flashed again and she saw him standing over her, the knife raised high. Kirsty grunted and slammed the knife down and buried it in Wilson's left foot. Wilson screamed in pain as the cabin went dark again.

Kirsty jumped to her feet and pushed out with both hands. She connected with his chest and she kept pushing and felt him fall backwards. She screamed as loud as she could and heard him fall to the floor. She stepped on his chest but stumbled as he rolled over and she fell against the cabin wall. The boat rocked and she pushed herself off the wall and she rushed towards the hatch.

She heard Wilson grunt and then there was another flash of lightning but she didn't turn around. He still had the knife and she wasn't sure how much damage she'd done to his foot.

"Kirsty, don't leave angry!" shouted Wilson. He started to laugh as her fingers scrabbled at the hatch and pulled it back. She felt a nail break as she pushed it back as far as it would go. "Kirsty!" roared Wilson, but she forced herself not to look around.

She scrambled up the stairs and screamed as she felt the knife tear across her back. She lashed out with her left leg, kicking backwards, and her foot connected with something and she heard him fall back and hit the floor.

She was exhausted but the adrenaline coursing through her bloodstream kept her going and she fell onto the deck and crawled along it. The blood from her wounds was mixing with the rain as she scrambled along on all fours. She threw herself off the boat and onto the pier, pushed herself up and started to run, her bare feet slapping against the wooden slats like gunshots.

CHAPTER 2

Dudley Grose walked into the lecture hall and swung his battered leather briefcase onto the table in front of the whiteboard. There was an overhead projector on the table but he never used it or the whiteboard. He'd long ago decided that he was there to talk and if the students didn't bother writing anything down then that was up to them. There was a wooden chair at the side of the table and he sat down and looked at the hundred or so students filling the rows of seats facing him. The keen ones were sitting at the front, their laptops open and primed, fingers poised over their keyboards. In the middle were the ones who took notes by hand, scribbling the odd phrase and chewing on the pens and nodding thoughtfully whenever they thought he was looking in their direction. At the back were the least-interested students, the ones who spent most of their time playing with their cell phones. Grose barely knew a dozen of them by name so he opened his briefcase and took out the folder in which he kept a printed list of the students who had signed up for the course, where they had come from, and what work if any they had handed in.

He stood up and the students fell silent. He was wearing a tweed jacket with leather patches on the elbows and green corduroy trousers and faded desert boots. Grose dressed for comfort and everything he was wearing he'd owned for at least ten years, even his socks and underwear.

He took a deep breath, trying to drum up the enthusiasm for a course that he had next to no interest in. 'The Mechanics Of Writing A Bestseller'. That hadn't been his choice. In fact he'd argued against it, pointing out that he was supposed to be teaching English Literature, not a Writing For Dummies course. He'd been over-ruled by the Head of the English Faculty, a pinch-faced lesbian who'd only been at the university for two years but who seemed to have it in for Grose and every other male member of staff aged over fifty. Grose was only a few months away from his fifty-second birthday. He didn't know if it was his age, sex or the patches on his jacket, that had annoyed her, but she'd seemed to have taken inordinate pleasure insisting on the title. She'd explained to him that it was all about pulling in the students, and that twenty-first century students weren't interested in studying the works of "long-dead white men" as she relished describing history's greatest writers.

Grose forced a smile as he surveyed the eager faces in the front row. "So, ladies and gentlemen, we now begin the third week of the course and as I told you on the first day, now is the time to put up, or shut up. Or as my old grandfather used to say, shit or get off the pot, God bless him."

He waited for laughter but there was none. Not even a smile. He looked over the top of his glasses. Without the benefit of corrective lenses everything beyond twelve feet was a soft blur and he generally found it less stressful addressing large groups of people when he couldn't see their faces.

"You all signed up for this course because you wanted to be writers, you wanted, for the lack of a better expression, to write the great American novel. I did hope that you might want to be the next Cameron Fitzgerald or Steinbeck or Hemingway or Salinger, but from the feedback I've been getting over the past two weeks it's clear that your sights are in the main somewhat lower. The new Stephanie Meyer, perhaps, or JK Rowling." His nose wrinkled as if he'd detected a bad smell wafting over from his audience. He took off his glasses and polished them with his handkerchief. The handkerchief had been a present from his wife many years ago and she'd embroidered his initials in blue in one corner. "But even if your ambitions are to pander to the mass market, you still have to do what all writers do – you have to write. You have to put words down on paper. Or I suppose these days the best I can hope is that you put them onto your hard disc drive." He put away his handkerchief but held onto his glasses. "Now, I might not be able to get you to write like Cameron Fitzgerald. I might not even get you to Stephanie Meyer standard, if indeed she has a standard, but the one thing I can guarantee you is peer review of your work, and that's something every writer needs. And today is the day that we start that process." He tucked the glasses in the top pocket of his jacket and opened the folder. He didn't need glasses for reading so long as he held the material at arm's length. "So, let's do this alphabetically, shall we? Miss Abrahams." He squinted at the students. "Miss Abrahams?"

A plump girl with badly-permed hair held up a hesitant hand. She smiled hesitantly. "That would be me."

Grose looked at his printout. "From Baltimore. Well Miss Abrahams from Baltimore, why don't you stand up and let us hear what you're working on."

"Now?"

"Now would be good, yes."

Her cheeks reddened. "It's not really ready for…" She shrugged. "It's just not ready."

"When do you think it will be ready?" said Grose.

"Next week?" she said, hopefully.

"What are you afraid of, Miss Abrahams? Ridicule? Contempt? Criticism? All of the above?"

Miss Abrahams slumped back in her seat and didn't answer. Grose took a step toward her. "That's what a writer does, Miss Abrahams. A writer bares his – or her –soul, a writer writes from the heart and then yes, that means opening yourself up to criticism. If you're not prepared to do that then you might as well go back to serving burgers or selling jeans or whatever it is you were doing before you let your dream of being a writer get the better of you. Do you understand me, Miss Abrahams?"

She nodded but didn't say anything and steadfastly refused to look him in the eye.

"I can't hear you," he said.

"Yes," she said, close to tears.

Grose sighed and looked around the lecture hall. "Very well," he said. "We'll drop the alphabetical system for today. By next Monday I want you all ready, willing and able to give the class a reading. It doesn't have to be much, a couple of pages will do. In the meantime, is there anyone who is ready now to bare their soul to the group?"

Several hands went up. The most enthusiastic was a blonde girl at the front who began waving her arm left and right like a metronome. Grose put on his glasses. The blonde was Melissa Knox, from Atlanta, big-boned and horse-faced, she had sat in the front row since day one of the course and was always the first to ask a question. Her voice was deep and throaty and for the first week he suspected that she might be a man in drag or at the very least a pre-op transsexual, but he'd come to accept that she was all woman. She was pushy, unpleasant, and seemed to think that she was destined to be heading the bestseller lists. She had already forced on him three writing samples which he'd read and dismissed as the product of a talentless wannabe writer, though of course he hadn't told her that. The Head of Faculty had made it clear that he was to be supportive and not critical, that the purpose of the course was to encourage creative development and not to be critical. Students didn't need to be criticized, he'd been told. They needed support. They needed encouragement. They needed smoke blown up their backsides is what she meant, but of course Grose hadn't told her that. He'd argued his case but that had been a waste of time. She'd taken him in to see the Dean.

The Dean was a forty-year old career academic who had never had an original thought in her head, so far as Grose could tell. She had a tight, birdlike face, close-cropped black hair and nails that were bitten to the quick. Her eyebrows had been shaped to within an inch of their lives and were always outlined with black pencil, and her lipstick was a pale beige that always seemed to find its way onto her front teeth. Kimberly Martin. Dean Martin. Under other circumstances Grose might have found the name funny, but there was nothing amusing about the Dean. She had backed the Head of Faculty, made a few patronizing comments about the university having to move with the times, and said that she was as pleased as punch with the number of students who had signed up for the course and didn't want him to do anything that would jeopordize those numbers.

Grose was pretty sure that Dean Martin was a lesbian and wouldn't have been at all surprised to learn that the Head of Faculty was her bitch. But he couldn't say that, of course. It was dangerous enough just to think it. In fact he was pretty sure that the day would come when even having a thought like that would lead to dismissal.

Melissa was bobbing up and down, her hand held high. Grose forced himself to smile, even though the last thing he wanted was to hear the silly woman's nauseating prose. "Yes, Melissa, let's start with you," he said.

Melissa was already on her feet. She picked up her MacBook, looked around to check that she had everyone's attention and began to read. Her voice seemed even deeper than usual and Grose couldn't help but look for signs of a prominent Adam's apple as she spoke.

Grose sat down and nodded thoughtfully as Melissa droned on. Her story was a soulless romance about a nurse in a mid-Western town who is torn between two men – an impossibly handsome doctor and an equally impossibly handsome delivery driver. Both had cleft chins, rippling muscles and washboard stomachs and both thought the nurse was the woman of their dreams. It was tosh. Absolute tosh. It was so bad that Grose was tempted to walk over, take the laptop from her and throw it against the wall. He settled for looking over at Jenny Cameron, another of the front row stalwarts. Jenny had been born in Orlando, not far from the Magic Kingdom, but whenever

Grose looked at her he imagined the sound of bagpipes and the smell of heather. Fair skinned, soft shoulder-length blonde hair and a sprinkling of faint freckles across her nose.

Grose continued to nod as he looked at Jenny, taking in her high cheekbones, Cupid's bow lips, pale blue eyes and long black eyelashes. She was the most beautiful woman he'd ever laid eyes on. Except she wasn't a woman, she was a girl. Less than half his age. A lot less than half, as it happened. Closer to a third. The thought made his stomach lurch.

She realized that he was looking at her and she smiled and self-consciously brushed a lock of hair behind her ear. Grose wanted to wink at her but he knew that wouldn't be smart, not with so many students facing him. He realized with a jolt that they were all looking at him expectantly and that Melissa had finished talking.

He smiled at her. "Excellent," he said. "First-rate." He took off his glasses again and slid them into his top pocket. "Now, let's all share our thoughts with Miss Knox. Who wants to start?" A forest of hands shot up.

CHAPTER 3

Grose carried his cup of coffee through into his study. Actually it was the spare bedroom at the rear of the house but he and his wife never had visitors and they'd never bothered to put in a bed. There was an old oak desk that he'd bought from an antiques shop in Maine shortly after they'd moved into the house. The desk had obviously once been in a large office as there was a small ivory button on one side which in the past had probably summoned an assistant or secretary. There were six drawers on either side and a wide drawer under the main section of the desk.

He opened the top left hand drawer, took out a yellow legal pad and sat back in his chair. The chair had cost more than four hundred dollars and was ergonomically designed to ensure the best possible sitting position and take the pressure off his spine. Grose had been troubled with back pain for almost ten years. The severity of the pain varied. Some days it was little more than an ache, at other times it was a searing burning sensation that brought tears to his eyes and prevented him from doing anything other than lying immobile on a hard surface until the agony faded. Painkillers hadn't helped and Grose had tried them all, from aspirin and codeine up to prescription drugs. He'd tried chiropractors and acupuncturists and once had even gone to a faith healer. Nothing worked, though the expensive chair did help.

He tapped his fountain pen against the pad. Grose always wrote by hand. It was the way Shakespeare wrote all his plays, the way that Dickens wrote all his masterpieces. If it was good for the masters, Grose figured that a pen and paper was good enough for him. He'd written all his novels by hand. All seven of them. For the last three he'd used the same Mont Blanc pen, filling it with fresh ink each morning. Once he'd finished the first draft his wife typed them into her computer and printed it out for him. He would then make any changes he wanted in pen and his wife would copy them onto the computer file. It normally took him eight or nine rewrites before he was happy, and at that point he would put the manuscript into the bottom drawer on the left of the desk and leave it there for four weeks. Exactly four weeks, never a day more or a day less. Then he'd take it out and try to read it as if he was seeing it for the first time. That was when the real revisions would start, and again he would do it by hand, laboriously rewriting line by line. His wife would type the new version into her computer and that would be followed by another five or six rewrites, each involving less work than the last until finally he had a version that he was truly happy with.

He looked down at the pad. He was on the twelfth page, which meant he had written just under three thousand words. He was finding it difficult to concentrate because he was still waiting to hear from his agent about the manuscript that he'd just finished the previous month. Grose sat back in his chair and looked up at the ceiling. It had been with the agent for two whole weeks and he still hadn't heard anything. It was the best thing he'd ever written, he was sure of that. As sure as he'd ever been about anything. He'd put his heart and soul into it, and he couldn't understand why it was taking his agent so long to get back to him.

Grose put down his pen, leaned back and stared at the phone, willing it to ring. Two weeks. Fourteen days. After three days he had phoned to check that the manuscript had arrived and a secretary had confirmed that it had. Actually manuscript was a misnomer. The agent had refused point blank to accept anything as old fashioned as paper. He'd insisted on Grose sending it by email, something which Grose detested. A book was paper, almost by definition, a thing of beauty that had to be held to be appreciated, not a stream of electrons whizzing across a screen. Grose could never understand anyone choosing to read or to write on a computer. Words needed to be on a page to be appreciated, to be savored. How was any agent supposed to make a considered decision by reading off a screen? Grose figured it was ridiculous, but that's what the man had insisted upon so Grose had asked his wife to email the file.

Grose had only met the man once. Richard Pink his name was, a partner in one of the bigger New York literary agencies. Pink was the third agent he had met and the only one who had come close to being acceptable. He was in his early thirties, sleek, bald and so well-groomed that Grose had assumed that the man was gay. He'd enthused about Grose's early work and had talked enthusiastically about movie deals and foreign rights and Grose had left the meeting feeling that a seven-figure-deal was just a few phone calls away. Pink had asked Grose what had happened to his last agent and Grose had explained that Bennie Knight had retired through ill-health. Bennie had always been a big man but in his seventies the weight had piled on and with it had come heart problems and diabetes and eventually he'd called it a day and retired to his house in the Hamptons. Bennie hadn't done much for Grose over the past ten years but at least he'd always stayed in touch, making a phone call every Monday morning, as regular as clockwork. "Just checking in, Dudley," he'd say, followed by exactly five minutes of small talk followed by a promise to stay in touch.

Pink didn't have Benny's charm or good humor but he did have energy and confidence and a Fifth Avenue office with windows on two sides. Grose had expected that Pink would have got back to him about the manuscript within twenty-four hours. Forty-eight at the most. After he'd phoned the secretary on the third day he was sure that Pink would be on the phone within hours, but no, he hadn't even had the decency to return the call. But now two weeks had passed. What was he playing at? Two weeks was more than enough time to read War and Peace from cover to cover and back again.

He picked up his fountain pen again and tried to write but he still couldn't concentrate. He reached for the phone and then shook his head. No, it wasn't his place to call. The ball was in Pink's court. He went down to the kitchen and made himself another cup of coffee. His wife was in the garden, down on her knees doing something to a spreading bush. She spent hours in the garden every day, rain or shine. It was a large garden, one of the main reasons they had bought the house, and over the twenty years they had lived there Karen had totally transformed it. There was a rose garden which produced prize-winning blooms, a water feature with a rocky waterfall, a small orchard and a vegetable patch that filled their larder all year round. It was a labor of love, Grose knew, and the more she had grown to love the garden the less attention she'd paid to him. The fact that they'd been unable to have children hadn't helped either. He shivered and turned away from the window.

He walked slowly back up the stairs and sat down at his desk. He picked up his pen, sucked on it for a while, and then put it down. He knew that he wouldn't be able to write a word until he knew one way or another where he stood with The Homecoming. He flicked through his FiloFax for the number of the agency, and then slowly tapped it out.

A receptionist answered and she put him through to Pink's secretary and she made him hold on the line for a full two minutes before putting him through.

"Dudley, hey, what's up?"

What's up? The words were like a slap across Grose's face. He'd sweated blood over The Homecoming, put almost two years of his life into writing it and three months polishing and editing it. What was up? The fact that the agent hadn't bothered to get back to him after two whole weeks was what was up. How long did it take to read a book? A day? Two days? Hell, a professional like Pink shouldn't take more than a few hours to read a manuscript. "No biggie, just calling to see if you had any thoughts on The Homecoming."

"The Homecoming?" repeated Pink and Grose felt his stomach lurch. The bastard couldn't even be bothered to remember the name of the book that had taken up more than two years of his life.

"The novel," said Grose, and hated himself as soon as the words had left his lips. "I emailed it two weeks ago."

"Sure, yes, The Homecoming," said Pink. "Brilliantly written, Dudley. Classic Dudley Grose. Classic."

Pink stopped speaking and Grose waited to see what he would say, but no more words came. The seconds ticked off.

Eventually Grose couldn't bear the silence any longer. "Did you have any thoughts?" he asked. He screwed up his face, realizing that he sounded like a schoolboy seeking praise for an essay.

"Right," said Pink, dragging the word out over several seconds, and Grose prepared himself. "Thoughts? Yes, well it flows well, the characters are memorable, some of the descriptions made me think of Roth at his best."

Grose clung to the compliment like a drowning man hanging on to a lifeline. "So you liked it?" he said.

There was silence for a few seconds and Grose was starting to wonder if the line had gone dead, but then he heard Pink cough quietly. "Hand on heart, Dudley, it's not the sort of book that I'm going to walk through walls for."

Grose frowned and slapped his hand against his forehead. What the hell did that mean? Walk through walls? Who the hell had suggested the agent try to defy physics? All he had to do was to send it out to the big publishers and start negotiations. How difficult was that ? Hell, he didn't even have to worry about postage, Pink could do it all with his precious email.

"I don't follow you," said Grose.

"It doesn't fire me up, Dudley. It doesn't get my pulse racing. And if I'm not passionate about a book I can't sell it. It would be dishonest of me to represent a book that I didn't love, and unfair to the writer. You need an agent who is prepared to go out and slay dragons for you and in this case I don't think I'd be up for slaying dragons."

Grose tightened his right hand into a fist and banged it against his forehead. He gritted his teeth and closed his eyes, fighting to contain the rage that was building up inside him. Slaying dragons? What was the moron talking about? "What are you saying, Richard?" said Grose, though he already knew what the agent meant. He was dropping him, like a stone. Or a turd. A turd was a better analogy. Pink thought the book was shit and he didn't want to touch it.

"It's just not my thing," said Pink. "Don't get me wrong. The writing is terrific. You are a great writer, one of great writers of the twentieth century."

"This is the twenty-first century, Richard."

"Exactly," said Pink. "And the world has moved on and I'm not convinced that the world of today is going to be queuing up to buy this novel. It's not what's selling."

"There are no vampires in it, is that it? Would you prefer a book with some stupid High School cheerleader torn between a vampire and a zombie? How about that?"

"Is that what you're working on now?" asked Pink without a trace of irony. "Sounds interesting, horror as literature, give it that Bram Stoker feel maybe. That could definitely work, Dudley."

Grose ground his knuckles into the bridge of his nose and he gritted his teeth again, harder this time. He wanted to scream obscenities at the man but he knew there was no point. It was his own fault for phoning. You only ever chased bad news. If it was good news it would come a-looking.

"Dudley, are you there?"

"I'm here, Richard," said Grose, struggling to keep his voice level. "And no, I'm not planning to start writing about vampires anytime soon."

"Vampires are hot," said Pink. "Zombies too. Teenagers can't get enough of them."

"I write for adults, not children," said Grose. "So what are you saying, Richard? The book needs work, is that it?"

"The book is wonderful, Dudley," said Pink. " It's classic Dudley Grose and I'm sure there'll be a publisher out there who'll bite your hand off but you need to find an agent who'll walk over burning coals for you."

"What does that mean?" said Grose. "Walk over burning coals? Why would you even say that? Why would I want you to walk over burning coals? I just need you to send out my book. How hard is that? I was nominated for a Pulitzer for God's sake. I've sold more than a million copies in sixteen languages."

"Yes but when?" said Pink. "Twenty-five years ago, right? How many are you selling now, Dudley? A thousand a year? Two thousand? Last time I looked two of your books aren't even in print."

"That's the publisher's fault," said Grose. "I keep pushing them to get my books back on the shelves but they don't listen."

"Because the market's changing," said Pink. "Bookshops are closing left right and center, Amazon is the king, and eBooks are what's happening now. You should think about that, Dudley. Seriously. Put your work up on Kindle and iBooks. That's where the readers are these days."

"Self-publish you mean," snorted Grose. He slumped back in his chair, knowing that the conversation was already over. He'd been dumped. His agent had fired him. "I'd rather shoot myself than start to publish my own work."

"Lots of writers are doing it," said Pink. "And not just new writers. Plenty of established writers are getting the rights to their backlist back and putting them on-line."

"I'm a writer," said Grose quietly. "I was nominated for a Pulitzer. I was featured in Time magazine. I topped the New York Times bestseller list for six months, Richard. Six months. I'm not going to start hawking my own work like some sort of snake oil salesman."

"I'm sorry you feel that way," said Pink. "Look, I'm going to have to rush, I've a conference call booked for ten. Good luck anyway. I'm sure you'll find someone to walk through..." He cut himself short. "There are plenty of agents out there who'd..."

Grose opened his mouth to swear at Pink, but then decided that it would be pointless. He put down the receiver without saying anything. He put his head in his hands, his eyes burning with tears of frustration. He was a writer, damn it. A Pulitzer-nominated writer who'd been featured on the cover of Time magazine. Who the hell was Pink, anyway? A middle-man, a Shylock taking fifteen per cent of whatever his clients earned. What did he know about writing? About constructing a novel, shaping a hundred thousand or more words into a structure that would keep a reader gripped for hours. The Homecoming was a good book, possibly a great book, and if Pink didn't appreciate that then he was an idiot.

"Honey? Are you okay?"

Grose took his hands away from his face and twisted around in his seat. His wife was standing in the doorway, taking off her gardening gloves. He forced himself to smile. "Damn agents," he said.

"Kill them all," she said. "Wasn't that what Shakespeare said?"

"He was referring to lawyers, but the principle's the same," said Grose. "Coffee?"

Grose looked at his watch. "I have to go," he said. "Tutorial."

"I thought you were off today?"

Grose stood up and took his jacket off the back of his chair. "It's an extra tutorial for the high-flyers," he said.

"Are you okay? You look... upset."

"Pink didn't like the book."

Her face fell and her look of concern made Grose feel suddenly ashamed. "Oh honey, I'm sorry."

He waved away her sympathy. "There are plenty of other agents," he said.

"Did he say why?"

"It wasn't his thing." He put on his jacket. "It doesn't matter."

"It does matter, Dudley. You put your heart and soul into that book. Two years work. Blood sweat and tears."

"Hardly that, Karen."

"How dare he turn you down? Who does he think he is?"

"A gatekeeper," said Grose. "You have to go through him or someone like him to get to the publishers and that gives them power."

"Why can't you send it to Random House? They published you before."

"Eric retired five years ago," said Grose. "I did speak to their head of publishing and she said that all submissions had to go through agents."

"Didn't she know who you are?"

"Of course she knew. But she didn't care."

"The world has gone mad," she said. "You almost got a Pulitzer. You sold millions of copies, they owe you."

"Publishing houses don't see it that way," said Grose. "She said I had to submit through an agent but..." He shrugged. "It doesn't matter."

She stepped forward and he knew that she was going to hug him. He put his hands up. "Karen, really, I'm not a kid."

She nodded. "Okay, I don't mean to fuss. It's not as if we need the money. You've got your job at the university, the house is paid for, we'll be fine."

"It's not about the money," said Grose. "It was never about the money. I just want people to read my work. To be moved by it. I'm a writer. That's what I do, I write. It's not my fault if an idiot like Pink wouldn't recognize a good book if it bit him on the ass."

"There are other agents, aren't there?"

"Sure. They're like cockroaches. My mistake was choosing a gay one."

She smiled. "I suppose the clue was in his name. Pink."

"I'm serious. The publishing business has been taken over by the gays and there aren't any gay characters in The Homecoming. Gay cowboys, that's what sells. Or gay private detectives. That and vampires and zombies and wizards." He looked at his watch again. "I have to go."

"We can talk about it over dinner. I'm doing sea bass. And I've some runner beans from the garden." She put a hand on his arm. "It'll be all right, Dudley. I know it will."

Grose saw the concern in her eyes and that only made him feel worse. He didn't want her sympathy. More importantly, he didn't need it. "I know," he said flatly. He picked up the car keys from the table in the hallway.

"Do you want me to drive you to the station?" she asked.

"Please, don't fuss over me," he said and hurried out, making a conscious effort not to slam the door behind him.

CHAPTER 4

Jenny looked up as the door buzzer rang. She frowned at the handset to the left of the front door and then looked at the clock in the top right hand corner of her laptop screen. It was just after mid-day and she wasn't expecting anybody. The door buzzer rang again, longer this time, but she ignored it. There were twenty apartments in the building and delivery men would often push buttons at random to get inside. "Go away," she muttered under her breath. "Writer at work."

She took a deep breath, trying to frame a paragraph that would describe the dress that her protagonist was wearing. She could describe people and places, but she never felt comfortable with clothes and furniture.

Her cell phone began to ring and she picked it up. She looked at the screen and smiled, then took the call. "Dudley, hi," she said. "What's up?"

"Where are you?"

"I'm at home," she said. "Writing."

"So why aren't you answering your doorbell?"

She laughed. "My God, is that you outside?"

"Of course it's me. Now are you going to let me in, or not?"

The intercom buzzed again. Jenny got up from the sofa and hurried over to the door. She picked up the receiver and pressed the button to open the door three floors below and then rushed into her tiny bathroom and put on fresh lipstick and squirted Coco on her neck. She was wearing an Emily the Strange t-shirt and black leggings but she didn't have time to change. She untied her hair and shook it loose before heading back to the door.

There were three locks and a chain to deal with and by the time she had the door open he was coming up the last flight of stairs.

"This is a nice surprise," she said.

"That was the idea," said Grose. He groaned and patted his chest. "You need an apartment with an elevator." He took a couple of deep breaths then walked inside and flopped down onto her sofa. "Are you working?" he asked, pointing at the laptop.

"You should have phoned," said Jenny, closing the door and clicking the locks shut. Her mother had made her promise on a Bible that she would always lock her door when she was in New York.

Grose looked over at her, his eyes narrowed. "What, now I need to make an appointment, do I?"

"Dudley, that's not what I meant," she said, dropping down on the sofa next to him and closing the laptop. She kissed him on the cheek. "If I'd known you were coming over I'd have worn something prettier."

Grose slipped his arm around her. "You look just perfect as you are," he said, and kissed her full on the lips. She straddled him and kissed him hard, grinding herself against him. He grunted as he stood up, holding her tightly, and she wrapped her legs around him.

"Dudley!"

He kissed her. "What?"

"What's come over you?"

"I missed you. I was going crazy at home."

"I missed you, too." She kissed him, hard, and squeezed her legs.

He grunted and carried her to the bedroom.

CHAPTER 5

Their lovemaking was over in less than ten minutes. Grose lay on his back, his arm around her, staring up at the ceiling. Jenny toyed with the hairs on his chest.

"Are you okay, Dudley?"

"Sure, honey, why?"

"You seem, I don't know, a bit tense."

He shrugged. "I'm fine," he said.

"Why did you come into the city today? I thought you had no classes today."

"I wanted to see you, is that so surprising?"

"You see me every day, silly," she said.

"Well, there's 'see' you and there's 'see' you, isn't there?" he said. "And today I really wanted to 'see' you."

"And everything's okay at home?"

"As ok as it ever is," he said.

"No problems with your wife?"

"She's fine. So long as she has her garden, she's happy."

"Leave her," she said. "You don't love her. You can move in with me."

Grose chuckled. "Live here, with you? We'd be at each other's throats in a week."

"Dudley, how can you say that?" She grabbed a handful of chest hair and tugged it.

He yelped and rolled away from her. "You know I can't walk out on her," he said. "She'd take everything."

"She'd take half of everything," she said, cuddling up to him again. "Living with me wouldn't cost you anywhere near as much as it costs for her. I don't need a garden, for one." She grinned. "Really, I'm low maintenance."

"Let me think about it," he said, but she could tell from his voice that he wasn't serious. It was the same tone that her father had used when he'd said that he'd think about getting her a pony. He looked at his watch. "Why don't we order Chinese?" he said. "I'm hungry."

"I feel a bit sick," she said. "I think I've got a stomach bug. I haven't felt like eating for a couple of days. But you go ahead."

"What about sandwiches then? From the deli on the corner?"

"I'm really not hungry, Dudley." She sat up and stretched. "What about going for a juice? I haven't been to the Elixir Juice Bar for ages."

"Honey, what if someone sees us? Come on now."

"So what if someone sees us? We'll just be having a juice? I wasn't planning on having sex with you there." She laughed. "Come on. It's a lovely day, let's go for a walk."

"Jenny, you know that if the faculty found out what was going on, I'd lose my job. You know that."

"So a student can't have a drink with her teacher?"

"I think we're beyond that," said Grose. "I just don't want people talking about us, that's all. We need to stay under the radar until you've graduated. Even then we have to be careful."

"Why?" asked Jenny.

Grose sighed. "You know why, honey. I'm a lecturer. You're a student."

"You've got hundreds of students."

"Yes, but I'm not sleeping with them, am I?"

"I hope not," she said, and pinched him around the waist.

"Don't!" he snapped.

"Don't worry, I won't mark you," she said. "I know the rules. No marks, no bites, no scratches."

"Jenny…"

"It's okay, Dudley." She kissed him on the shoulder. "You should just leave her. Your marriage is dead, you said it was, and it's not as if you've got kids." She stroked his chest. "I'm serious, Dudley. You can move in here."

"Your parents would kill me."

"Not after I've told them that we love each other."

"Jenny, honey, I'm older than your dad."

"Not by much. And you're nothing like him."

He kissed the top of her head. "He'd come looking for me with a shotgun."

"No he wouldn't."

"And even if he didn't shoot me, I'd lose my job. There's no way they'd let me continue teaching there if I was living with a student."

She sat up, her eyes flashing. "So quit," she said excitedly. "You hate teaching anyway."

"That's not true, honey."

"You moan about the students, you moan about the Head of Faculty, you moan about the Dean. Name me one thing about the university that you like."

"You," he said.

Jenny giggled. "I knew you'd say that," she said. "But that's the point. You can have me without having to teach. You're going to make a fortune from The Homecoming. Once the publishers have seen it there'll be a bidding war and they'll pay you millions and you won't have to teach." She snuggled against him. "Then you can just stay with me and write your next bestseller."

"Sounds like a plan," said Grose.

"It is a plan," said Jenny. "The perfect plan. If you get big bucks for The Homecoming you can let your wife have anything she wants. You'll have more than enough money."

"I guess so," said Grose.

"Have you heard from that agent yet?"

"No, not yet," Grose lied.

"What's taking so long?"

"I don't know," said Grose, fighting to keep the bitterness from his voice.

"It's a masterpiece," said Jenny. "It's bound to be a bestseller, they must see that." She kissed his shoulder. "How long has it been? Three weeks?"

"Two," said Grose. He felt tears welling up in his eyes and he blinked them back.

"Maybe you should call him. Tell him you want to get it sent to publishers as soon as possible."

"Maybe I will," said Grose.

"Everything's going to work out, Dudley," she said. "I can feel it in my bones. Really, I can."

"Of course it will," he said. He sighed. "I really do want some Chinese, you know. Can you call that place I like? The one that does the fried prawn thing?"

CHAPTER 6

Grose polished his glasses and tried to concentrate on what the student was reading from the laptop in front of her. Her name was Sadie Wilkinson and she was wearing a baggy flower-patterned dress that made her look like an over-stuffed sofa. There were thick rolls of fat around her neck and her arms were the size and texture of hams but she did have a pretty face. Grose found his mind wandering again and he wondered why Sadie didn't just take a look in the mirror and cut her calorific intake in half. He put his glasses back on and caught Jenny smiling at him. He flashed her a quick smile and then turned his attention back to Sadie. She was in full flow, her cheeks were flushed and there were beads of sweat on her forehead.

"Laura pressed against her, soft and wet, like no woman had ever kissed her before. Her insistent fingers probed deep into her secret places, touching, caressing, coaxing her on and on until she burned within. She wanted to give her all to Sonya, to open herself wide, wider than she'd ever opened herself to anyone. She wanted to tell Sonya that there wasn't anything she wouldn't do for her. Anything."

The last few sentences had come out in a single burst and Sadie had to take a deep breath.

Grose could see that several of the men in the audience were staring at Sadie, their eyes wide and mouths open.

Sadie smiled nervously. "That's all I've got so far," she said.

One of the male students groaned and sat back, a look of disgust on his face.

"Interesting," said Grose. "Any comments?"

Jenny was the first to raise her hand and Grose nodded at her. "Yes, Miss Cameron?"

"I thought it was a clever use of narrative. I really felt like I got inside her."

There were a few giggles from the students at the back of the lecture hall.

"I mean, inside the head of the main character," Jenny added quickly. "You really got to feel her emotions."

That's good, Jenny," said Grose. "Good feedback." He looked around the class. "Anything else?" All he could see were blank faces and the only student who would look him in the eye was sitting right at the back. A man in his mid-twenties, black gelled hair and RayBans. He took notes the old fashioned way, with a pencil and notepad. Grose took a quick look at his list of students. Adrian Slater from Los Angeles. "What about you, Mr Slater? I don't think we've heard from you yet. What did you think of Miss Wilkinson's work in progress?"

Slater held Grose's look for several seconds and then he nodded slowly and put down his notepad. "It certainly got you inside the head of the main character," he said. "Personally I'd have liked some dialogue rather than only getting the scene from the protagonist's viewpoint. But I'm not sure how marketable the story would be, as a novel."

"And should that be a concern?" asked Grose.

"Whether or not a story will sell? Sure. Isn't that the whole point of writing? To sell."

Grose tilted his head on one side as he looked up at Slater. "Is that how you judge quality, Mr Slater? By sales?"

"What other way is there of assessing a book's success?"

Grose chuckled. "Well, there's the quality of the writing for instance. Sales have nothing at all to do with quality. Who can tell me what the best-selling book of all time is?" He looked around the lecture hall and nodded at a blonde-haired young man in an NY Yankees baseball jacket who had raised his hand.

"Yes?" asked Grose.

"The Da Vinci Code?" said the student, and he flinched at the laughter that echoed around the room.

Grose shook his head sadly. "Enlighten us, Miss Cameron," he said.

"The Bible," she said, on cue.

"Exactly," said Grose, looking up at Slater. "The Bible. Closely followed by the Koran. Neither of which are considered to be well written. And while A Tale of Two Cities has sold two hundred million copies and is indeed a classic, it's also the case that Agatha Christie's crime novel And Then There Were None has sold over one hundred million and it's a terrible book." He looked over at the student in the baseball jacket. "And yes, the Da Vinci Code also sold well, more than eighty million I believe, and yet it falls well short of being a competent novel, never mind a classic. Sales are no guide to quality, Mr Slater."

Slater nodded thoughtfully but said nothing.

"I get the feeling that you don't agree with me, Mr Slater."

"It's your course, Doctor Grose."

"That doesn't preclude you from having an opinion, does it?"

"I guess not," said Slater. He put his pencil down on top of his notebook and leaned forward, interlinking his fingers. He took a deep breath as if composing himself. "It seems to me that the rules have changed and it's ePublishing that's changed it."

"Ah," said Grose. "You're a Kindle convert? Publishing is dead, long live eBooks?"

"Before long the eBook market will be many times the market for dead tree books," said Slater. "And anyone can publish an eBook. You don't need an agent or a publisher, all you need is a laptop and you can put your work out to the worldwide market. And whereas in the old days the agents and publishers were the gatekeepers, now it's the buyers who decide what sells and what doesn't. So the idea of producing quality work has gone out of the window. Now all that matters is how many you sell."

"You seriously believe that?" asked Grose. "You seriously think that the only worth of a book is how many it sells?"

"What else is there? Pulitzers?"

Grose's jaw tightened.

"The Nobel prize?" asked Slater. "Are awards the way we should value books? Awards are political as much as anything and have nothing to do with quality."

"So you let the people choose, is that it? Writers are selected by popular vote, like some sort of literary American Idol?"

"Maybe," said Slater.

"Maybe? So you can see the day when writers pitch their stories to the likes of Simon Cowell and Piers Morgan and then America votes to decide the winner. Which means that writers begin to pander to the lowest common denominator. How sad would the world be then, Mr Slater?"

"I guess it depends on your view of what writing is," said Slater.

Grose frowned. "I don't follow you."

Slater shrugged and unlinked his fingers. "Is a writer's function to produce work of quality, or to produce work that sells? Because speaking personally I would rather sell a million copies than get a Pulitzer."

"Perhaps you could do both," said Grose, though he didn't for one moment believe that Slater was capable of that.

"But does the Pulitzer matter? In the grand scheme of things, aren't a million sales better than any award?"

"Are you asking me, Mr Slater, or is your question rhetorical?"

"It's rhetorical because I think the answer is obvious." He looked around for support and several students were nodding in agreement.

"Perhaps you would be so good as to give us a sample of your writing, Mr Slater?"

Slater looked pained. "I don't have it with me," he said.

"That's a pity," said Grose. "Can you at least tell us the title? Do you have one?"

"The Bestseller," said Slater. Several of the students laughed and Grose saw Jenny twist around in her seat to look up at Slater. He felt a sudden twinge of jealousy and he gritted his teeth. Slater held up his hands, smiling good naturedly. "I know, I know, but I figured there was no point in hiding my light under a bushel."

"Perhaps you'd be good enough to bring in your work in progress tomorrow," said Grose. "Then the class can let you know whether you really do have a bestseller on your hands."

Slater sat back in his seat and put his pen down on his notepad. "Can I ask you something, Doctor Grose?"

"What?"

"Could we perhaps hear you read something you've been working on?"

Grose said nothing but his eyes narrowed.

"I mean, you haven't published a book in what, seven years? Nothing since The Brothers McFee, right? And your last big seller was Snow Birds and that was twenty-odd years ago. The one that was nominated for the Pulitzer. I think we'd all like to hear what you're working on now."

Grose swallowed. His mouth had gone dry. He coughed to cover his discomfort "This course is about helping you to improve as writers," he said. "The last thing I want to do is to have you listen to my work."

"But Snow Birds sold half a million copies, and was nominated for a Pulitzer," said Slater. "You managed to combine quality with quantity."

"That's nice of you to say so, Mr Slater, but as I said, this course is about you and your fellow students."

"But you are working on something, aren't you?" pressed Slater. "Writer's write, that's what you said on the first day. Writing to a writer is like breathing, you said, it's something you do."

Grose took off his glasses and began polishing them.

"Is it because you're worried that you might have peaked when you were thirty and that you'll never write as good a book again?"

Grose put his glasses back on and shoved the handkerchief in his pocket. He looked at his watch pointedly. "Let's call it a day, shall we. You can all use the time to work on your projects, and you Mr Slater, tomorrow we will all listen to your bestseller and see if it lives up to its name."

Grose picked up his briefcase. As he walked out he flashed Jenny a quick smile but she wasn't looking at him, she had twisted around in her seat to get a better look at Slater.

CHAPTER 7

Grose dropped his briefcase onto the table and turned to survey the class. He flashed Jenny a quick smile and then looked towards the back of the class. Slater was there, his eyes hidden behind impenetrable RayBans. The students fell silent. The overzealous ones already had their fingers poised over their laptops, ready to take down his every word. "I hope you're all progressing with your work," he said, taking off his glasses and polishing them. "Because that is what this course is about. It's only by putting one's work up for peer review that one can improve. And a writer who doesn't improve will stagnate and die. So criticism is not to be feared or even resented, it is to be welcomed with open arms." He put his spectacles back on and looked up at the back row. "So with that in mind, is Mr Slater now ready to share his work in progress with us?"

Slater put down his notepad and pencil then stood up and looked around the lecture hall, like a gladiator surveying the Coliseum. "Ready as I'll ever be," he said.

"And is it still titled The Bestseller?"

"It is," said Slater. He bent down to pick up a backpack and took out several sheets of paper held together with a large bulldog clip.

"I admire your confidence," said Grose. He sat down, crossed his legs, and motioned for Slater to begin.

Slater took a deep breath, lifted his chin, and began to speak. "I'd kill to write a bestseller," he said. He spoke loudly and clearly and his words carried across the lecture hall but most of the students frowned as if they weren't sure what they had just heard. Slater paused for effect before continuing. "I can write. I know I can write. But being a writer isn't enough for me. I want to be the best, the most successful, the most commercial. I want to sell a million copies. I want to be famous, all around the world."

He paused again and looked at Grose, then smiled. Grose stared back impassively.

"But what I need to succeed is a gimmick," Slater continued. "A unique selling point. Something that will seize the public's imagination. I have that unique selling point, I know how to write a book that will sell like no other book has sold before. I will - literally - kill to write a best-seller."

"Mr Slater, what is this?" asked Grose.

Slater ignored the interruption and carried on reading. "So here's what I'll do. I'll choose a victim, someone at random. I'll write about her - yeah, it'll have to be a girl - then I'll kill her. Not for pleasure, not for the kick, but for the book. The bestseller."

Several of the students began whispering among themselves and those at the front were twisting around in their seats to get a better view of Slater.

"I'll describe everything in the book. What I did, how I did it, but I won't say who the girl was or where the body is buried. But there'll be clues in the book, clues that'll tell where the body is."

"Mr Slater!" said Grose. "What are you doing?"

Slater looked up from his papers. "What?"

"I said what are you doing?"

Slater frowned. "I'm reading my novel."

"That is not a novel."

Slater put his head on one side. "It is. It's what I've been working on."

"But it's not a novel. It's…" Grose threw up his hands. "I don't know what it is, but it's not a novel."

"It's my work in progress," said Slater. "It's setting the scene for what comes next."

"But the narrator is you, correct?"

Slater shook his head. "No."

"I'm confused, Mr Slater. The narrator is talking about writing a bestseller?"

"Yes."

"And that he's going to kill to achieve that aim?"

"That's right."

"But that's not you?"

"The narrator? Of course not. Can I carry on?"

Grose waved a languid hand but didn't say anything.

Slater took a breath, and began to read again. "The trick, of course, is to get everybody talking about the book. Word of mouth is what sells. A buzz, they call it. And what better way to create a buzz than to tell everyone that I've committed the perfect murder. I'll reveal everything. I'll explain how I chose the victim, how I carried out the murder, and how I disposed of the body. I'll describe my feelings, I'll explain what goes through your mind when you take a life, what it feels like to see a human being die in front of you. I still haven't chosen the weapon. A gun is too easy, too quick, too impersonal. It doesn't take any skill to kill with a gun. You point and pull the trigger and the technology does the work. A knife maybe. A knife is personal. You have to get close, so close that you can look the victim in the eye as their lifeblood drains away. And the victim. That's the really important choice, of course. Who do I kill? Whose life do I take?"

"Enough, Mr Slater!" shouted Grose. He got to his feet and walked up the stairs to where Slater was standing.

"What's the problem?"

Grose took the sheets of paper from Slater. "This!" he shouted. "This is the problem!"

"I don't understand why you're so upset," said Slater. He sat down and folded his arms.

"You were supposed to be writing a novel," said Grose. He removed the bulldog clip and held up the papers. "This is garbage. A novel is a work of fiction. This, this is… I don't know what this is."

"It is a novel," said Slater. "First person narrative. Maybe it's the structure you don't like?"

"It's not about structure. Good God man, what are you thinking?" Slater didn't answer. "You're supposed to be writing a novel. A story with a beginning, a middle and an end. This isn't a novel. This is…." He struggled to find the right word. "Sick," he said eventually. "This is sick."

"The narrator's sick. That's the point."

"The point?" echoed Grose.

"The point of the book. The narrator's sick."

"But you're the narrator."

"What?"

"It's your voice. You're the narrator."

Slater shook his head. "I'm the writer," he said. "Writing with the narrator's voice. It's like American Psycho. Bret Easton Ellis."

"I know who wrote American Psycho, Mr Slater," said Grose. "Terrible book."

"It sold millions, though. And it was written from the viewpoint of a psychopathic serial killer."

"So that's what you're doing, copying another writer's story? There's a word for that, Mr Slater. Plagiarism." He handed the papers back. "Can I suggest you rethink this, Mr Slater. The purpose of this course is to produce quality work, work that one day might be publishable. You're wasting your time, my time, and the class's time with this drivel."

Grose was about to walk back to his table when he spotted Slater's notepad. It was open at a drawing. Grose frowned and picked up the notepad. Slater tried to take it from him but Grose moved the pad away from him. It was a caricature. A man in a tweed jacket with patches on the elbows sitting at a typewriter. Above his head was a balloon filled with question marks. The man had a weak chin and lines across his forehead and heavy bags under his eyes and he looked tired, as if the world was treating him badly and he expected the treatment to get worse. Grose felt his heart began to pound but he resisted the urge to snap at Slater. Everyone was looking at him and he'd gain nothing by losing his temper. "Very amusing, Mr Slater," said Grose, tossing the pad down. "Perhaps if you spent more time writing and less time doodling you'd be able to produce better work. But somehow I doubt it."

Grose walked back to his table, feeling the eyes of his class boring into his back. He took off his glasses and turned to face them. He forced a smile. "Right, who else has something they want to share with the class? Hopefully something more akin to a novel this time."

CHAPTER 8

Slater was on the sidewalk when Jenny walked out of the Arts Faculty building. She smiled and he smiled back. "Well I liked it," she said.

"What?"

"Your work in progress. It was cool."

"Thanks." He was carrying a black motorcycle helmet and had a backpack slung across one shoulder.

"You've got a bike?"

"Nah, I just like wearing the helmet," he said, and grinned when he saw her face fall. "Yeah, I've got a bike." He was wearing his shades and she could see herself reflected in both lenses.

"A Harley?"

Slater laughed. "Why does everyone always assume that if you've got a bike you've got a Harley? Harleys are heavy and slow and handle like refrigerators. Harleys are for dentists who want something big between their legs on weekends."

"So what do you have?" she said. She grinned slyly. "Between your legs on weekends?"

"A Kawasaki," he said. "A big one."

"There you see, I was always told that size isn't everything."

"Is that so? Because I was always told not to believe everything I was told." He winked at her and headed off.

She hesitated for a second, then hurried after him. He didn't look at her as she fell into step beside him. "I can see what you're trying to do," she said. "Shock tactics. Grab the reader by the throat and don't let go."

Slater didn't say anything.

"How many words do you think it'll be?" she asked.

He shrugged. "As many as it takes. It's like asking how long's a piece of string."

"That's easy," said Jenny. "It's twice as long as the distance from the end to the middle." Slater didn't react, he just kept on walking purposefully, but not so quickly that she couldn't match his pace. "I guess you never know how long a book's going to be until you finish it, right?"

"Have you finished writing a book yet?"

Jenny laughed. "I wish. I've rewritten my opening chapter a dozen times. More than that. Fifty, maybe."

"You're striving for perfection, is that it?"

"I just know that it's not right. It's like I know when it's wrong but I don't know how to put it right." She clasped her laptop case to her chest. "I guess that's why I'm on the course. To become a better writer."

"Yeah, well I'm not sure that Grose is gonna help you with that," he said. "The man's an idiot." He stopped walking and looked at his watch, a chunky diver's model with a numbered bezel.

"Have you got to be somewhere?"

He shrugged carelessly. "Wondering whether to go home or to get a coffee."

" Coffee sounds good," she said.

He looked at her and frowned. "That wasn't me trying to hit on you," he said. "You realize that?"

Jenny laughed. "Yeah, I didn't notice any subtext," she said. "Anyway, we've already met cute. So coffee is just coffee." She realized that she was hugging her laptop case close to her chest and she forced herself to relax.

"Met cute?" he said. "You believe in that crap?"

"I was joking, Adrian."

"Yeah, but you know that meeting cute is the prelude to characters getting together. It's such a cinematic cliché. Act One they meet cute, Act Two obstacles are placed in their way, Act Three they overcome the obstacles and live happily ever after." He shook his head in disgust. "It's writing by numbers. The same formula followed by millions of wannabe writers."

Jenny shrugged. "Rain check on the coffee, then," she said, and started to walk away. She felt her cheeks reddening and she lowered her head and let her hair fall across her face.

"Jenny!" he called after her but she pretended not to hear him and carried on walking. He hurried after her. "Wait," he said.

She didn't stop and didn't look across at him when he fell into step behind her. "I'm sorry. I get a bit carried away sometimes. It's just I know I can write, but I keep coming up against idiots like Grose who tell me there's only one way to write and that it's their way or the highway."

"I understand," said Jenny.

"You do?"

"I'm not stupid."

"I know you're not stupid. I didn't mean that." He chuckled softly. "This has gone from meeting cute to hating each other at first sight."

"I don't hate you," she said.

"I was being ironic. Really." There was a Starbucks ahead of them. "Can I at least buy you a coffee?"

"You sure?"

"Sure I'm sure. You can tell me how good you thought my story was."

"Now that's more like it."

"More like what?"

"Irony," she said. "Okay, you can buy me coffee."

They went into the coffee shop. Slater ordered an Americano and Jenny asked for a latte. "Do you want a muffin or a sandwich?" he asked.

She patted her stomach. "I don't feel so great," she said. "My stomach's been off for a few days. I think there's a bug going around. Just coffee. Latte. Low fat milk."

"Hold this for me, yeah," he said, and handed her the motorcycle helmet. She took it over to a table by the window and sat down and waited for him. He carried over the coffees. "I figured you didn't take sugar," he said.

"You figured wrong." She laughed. "I'll get it." As Slater sat down she went over and got herself two packets of sugar and a plastic spoon. Slater was staring through the window at the passers-by when she got back to the table.

"I didn't mean to upset you, before," he said.

"You didn't upset me."

"It came out wrong. I didn't mean that you wrote by numbers. I was trying to be funny but sometimes I say things without thinking."

"You're passionate," she said as she sat down. "Passion is good. Without passion you might as well be writing an instruction manual."

He nodded, still looking out through the window. "I don't think Grose sees it that way."

"He's a different sort of writer," she said. "He's more cerebral."

Slater snorted softly, then rubbed the bridge of his nose. "Cerebral? That's one way of putting it." He picked up his coffee and sipped it. "So what's your novel about?"

"It's nothing," she said.

"Nothing?" His eyes sparkled with amusement. "You're writing about nothing?"

She felt her cheeks redden. "It's not that. I just don't like talking about it."

"Why?"

She shrugged. "I don't know. Maybe I'll jinx it."

He sipped his coffee again. "Don't tell me the specifics then. Just generally."

Jenny nodded thoughtfully. "Okay," she said. "It's a romance."

"Romance is good," he said. "Just don't tell me there are vampires in it."

"Of course not," she said. "It's about a girl who works in a diner, waiting tables. She has a boyfriend who's a mechanic but he isn't the best boyfriend in the world. Blue collar, loves his truck more than her, drinks too much."

"A regular Joe."

"Exactly."

"And definitely not a vampire? Or a werewolf?"

She giggled and put her hand up to cover her mouth.

"Don't do that," he said.

"Do what?"

"Cover your mouth when you laugh. You look pretty when you laugh, you should let the world see it."

Jenny shook her head. "I don't know how you do that. How can you say exactly what you're thinking?"

"I can't be bothered with bullshit, Jenny," he said. "Life's too short to be anything less than honest." He sipped his coffee again, then pointed at the gold charm bracelet on her right wrist. "That's interesting," he said.

She held out her arm so that he could get a better look. It was a thick gold chain dulled by age and from it were hanging a dozen small charms. "It was my grandmother's," she said. "She died two years ago and she left it to me."

"I'm sorry," said Slater. He flashed her a tight smile. "Sorry that she passed away, I mean. Not sorry that she gave you the bracelet. It's pretty." He held one of the charms between his thumb and forefinger. "Is this a Bible?"

Jenny nodded. "A miniature one. You can open it and there are the words of the Lord's Prayer. It's more than a hundred years old, she said. It belonged to her mother. So did the chain." She shook her wrist. "It's really heavy."

"Must be worth a fortune," he said. "You should be careful, wearing that in the city."

"I hadn't thought of that," she said. "I'd hate to lose it. Every one of the charms meant something to my Gran. The Bible because she was a Christian. There's a small pair of scissors because she worked as a seamstress when she was a teenager. There's a heart that her husband gave her on the day she was married. There's a crib that granddad got her the day my mom was born. There's a small Eiffel tower she got after they went on a vacation to France, a ship to celebrate when they went on the Queen Mary and a steering wheel because she used to drive around in an old Volkswagen Beetle. Every one of them meant something to her."

"That's wonderful," he said. He was holding her hand as he studied the charms and he looked up and smiled.

Jenny smiled back but then felt her cheeks suddenly redden and she pulled back her hand.

"So have you really just done one chapter?" asked Slater, picking up his coffee.

"I don't want to start the second until the first one is perfect. Dudley says that…" She looked down at her cup.

"Dudley?"

"Doctor Grose, I mean."

"But you said Dudley. Is he Dudley to you, Jenny?" Slater leaned across the table towards her. "OMG," he whispered. "Dudley and Jenny, sitting in a tree…"

"It's not like that," she said, but she could feel her cheeks going bright red. She had always blushed when she was embarrassed, ever since she was a toddler.

"You're secret's safe with me," said Slater. "If you and Cuddly Dudley have a thing going on, it's none of my business."

"There's no secret," she said. "And no thing. He's married."

"Being married doesn't mean anything," said Slater. "But like I said, your secret's safe with me."

"Stop saying that," she said. "There's no secret. It was a slip of the tongue." She looked up at him, her eyes pleading. "Can we just change the subject?" She forced a smile. "So is this bestseller thing your first novel?"

"No," said Slater. "I'm not a virgin." He grinned.

"How many have you written?"

"A few," said Slater. He looked around. "I could do with a cigarette."

"You smoke?"

"Sure. Doesn't everybody?"

"You're not worried about cancer?"

"Jenny, I could get hit by a bus tomorrow. And I like smoking." He finished his coffee. "Do you want to go for a walk? In the park? I can smoke and I'll tell you about the book I've just finished."

"You're not allowed to smoke in the parks in New York. How can you not know that?"

"I'm not from here, remember. How the hell did they get away with telling New Yorkers they can't smoke outdoors?"

"It's the law."

"Smoking dope's against the law, are you telling me you've never even tried a joint? And using a cell phone while you're driving, you've never done that? And how old were you when you first had a drink?"

"You're a rebel, aren't you?"

"Now you're being sarcastic. I just don't think anyone had the right to tell me I can't enjoy a cigarette outdoors. It's nonsense." He gestured at the park. "Come on, let's go break the law. You can be a rebel, too."

CHAPTER 9

Slater put his motorcycle helmet down on the grass, used a battered Zippo to light a cigarette and then blew a tight plume of smoke into the air with a look of contentment on his face. He held out the pack of cigarettes but she shook her head. He slowly looked around the towering blocks that overlooked the park and smiled. "New York always brings out the serial killer in me," he said quietly.

"What?" said Jenny.

Slater chuckled softly and took another long drag on his cigarette. "It's the first line of the book I've just finished," he said.

"Not the one you were talking about in class? The Bestseller?"

"No, The Bestseller is a work in progress. The serial killer one is called The Basement. The central character is a guy by the name of Marvin Waller and that's the first thing you hear him say in the book."

"That's not the one you were reading from. In class?"

Slater shook his head. "The Bestseller isn't written yet. It's a work in progress. That was always the idea, to read out what I was writing and then incorporate the reaction it gets into the story."

"So you'll be writing about Dudley?"

"About everybody. That's the point."

"You mean I'll be in the book?"

"Sure."

"And this conversation we're having? Will that be in the book."

Slater grinned. "It's not a diary," said Slater. "Only stuff that's relevant to the plot will go in. The plot's got to keep moving otherwise there's no story. What about you? Do you keep a diary?"

"Why do you ask that?"

"You look like the sort who'd keep a diary, that's why. A lot of writers do. It's a way of collecting thoughts that you can use in your writing."

"You're right. I've always kept a diary, ever since I was a kid."

"A pink one with a padlock?"

Jenny laughed. "When I was six, yes. Now I use a proper notebook."

He held out the pack of cigarettes again. "I'm not a smoker, Adrian," she said. "Never have and never will. So this book that you've finished. It's about a serial killer?"

"Yeah. Sort of."

"Sort off?"

"It's complicated," said Slater. "I've tried to keep the reader guessing."

"But it's written from the viewpoint of the killer, you said. So it's like American Psycho as well?"

"Now that would be a spoiler, Jenny. I'll let you read it some time. Anyway, Waller is a wannabe screenplay writer who isn't having much luck selling his movies. Truth be told, he isn't a great writer but he thinks he is. He just figures that if he can get his screenplay on the right desk he'll be rich and famous."

"That much is true," said Jenny. "It's all about getting your work read by the right people. If you can't get an agent you can't get a publishing deal. And agents are really hard to get to."

"I'm sure Dudley will help get your book out there," said Slater, and he picked up his mootorcycle helmet and started walking across the park.

Jenny hurried after him. "What do you mean?"

"You know what I mean," said Slater. "Grose has contacts, he knows agents, he can get your work read."

"I'm not sleeping with him!"

Slater stopped walking and looked at her with a broad smile on his face. "Did I say you were?"

"You're inferring it."

"I might be implying it, but I'm definitely not inferring it," said Slater.

"What?" said Jenny, confused.

"It doesn't matter," said Slater. "I just said that Grose should be able to help you. He's got contacts. You're the one who mentioned sleeping. The lady do protest too much, methinks."

"What do you mean?"

"Shakespeare. Hamlet Act 3, Scene 2. Most people misquote it and say "methinks the lady do protest too much" but as usual most people would be wrong."

"You read Shakespeare?"

"Jenny, you can't be a writer without knowing the classics. Shakespeare, Dickens, Hardy. Grisham." He grinned. "I'm joking about Grisham."

He started walking again and Jenny fell into step next to him. "I'm really not sleeping with him."

"Good."

"Why good?"

"Because he'd be abusing his authority and it'd cost him his job, tenure or no tenure."

"Anyway, he's married."

Slater flicked ash from his cigarette. "Oh sure, married men never sleep around." A woman pushing a toddler in a stroller glared at him as he smoked his cigarette. Slater grinned at her and held up the cigarette. "It's not real, ma'am. It's plastic. One of those new-fangled artificial ones."

The woman looked away and hurried down the path.

"See that?" he said to Jenny. "Why do people hate smokers so much?"

"Smoking kills people," said Jenny.

"Smoking kills smokers," said Slater. "It's a choice."

"There's secondary smoke."

"I'm outside, in a park," he said. "A park surrounded by roads full of cars belching fumes that are far more poisonous than this." He held up his cigarette. "The average New York taxi cab puts out more pollution in a day than I'll cause in a lifetime of smoking. And the jury's out on secondary smoking. Trust me, I've looked at the evidence and there isn't any. You breathe in more toxins walking down Sixth Avenue than you do living with a smoker."

He walked off the path and onto the grass. Jenny followed him. "I lied when I said I've never smoked," she said. "I tried it once. It made me cough."

Slater laughed. "How old were you?"

"Fifteen."

"You rebel. It makes everyone cough the first time. It's like coffee. No one really likes their first coffee. It's an acquired taste." He sat down on the grass, put down his backpack and motorcycle helmet, then took out his pack of cigarettes, flicked it open and offered it to her.

She stood looking down at him, frowning, then realized that he wanted her to take one. "Oh no, I can't," she said.

"Of course you can. You tried when you were fifteen. You can try again now."

"I don't want to."

"You don't want to? Or are you being told that you mustn't? You're scared of the disapproval of the sour-faced hag pushing her ugly offspring around in his five-hundred dollar stroller? Think what her carbon footprint is? Her banker husband probably drives a Ferrari and they fly first class to the Bahamas twice a year and let's not get started on all the electrical appliances they have in the duplex in Park Avenue."

"You know her?"

"I'm guessing," said Slater. He jiggled the pack at her. "It's your life, Jenny. Your body. Your soul. It's up to you to make your own decisions, you can't let everyone else tell you how to run your life."

Jenny bit down on her lower lip and then hesitantly reached out and took a cigarette.

"Good girl," said Slater, putting the backpack and motorcycle helmet onto the grass and holding up his lighter. He flicked the thumb wheel and she bent down and lit the cigarette from the smoky flame. She straightened up and almost immediately began coughing. She patted her chest with her left hand and grinned ruefully as she blinked away tears.

"I told you, it's an acquired taste," said Slater. He patted the grass next to him. "Come on, sit down."

Jenny sat down next to him, crossed her legs and took a slow pull on the cigarette but after just a few seconds she started to cough again. She put her hand over her mouth as she coughed, then shook her head. "I can't," she said.

"Take it slowly," said Slater. "And give the nicotine a chance to work its way through your bloodstream."

"You're the devil, aren't you?" said Jenny, looking at the cigarette as if seeing it for the first time. "I can't believe you've got me smoking."

"You have to try everything, at least once," said Slater. He lay back and stared up at the sky. "We're writers, Jenny. We write about the human condition. If you write about a character smoking, then you have to know what it feels like to smoke a cigarette. If you want to write about getting drunk then you have to know what it's like to be drunk." He blew a plume of smoke up into the air and watched the wind whisk it away. "Do you think a virgin could write about making love?"

Jenny lay down on the grass. Overhead there was a puffy white cloud in the shape of a duckling.

"Well?" said Slater.

"Well what?"

"Can a virgin write about sex?"

"If she has a good imagination, maybe."

"Nonsense," said Slater dismissively. "You have to do it before you can write about it. You have to write from experience."

Jenny took a careful pull on her cigarette and held the smoke deep in her lungs. She could feel it, almost like a living thing, deep in her chest, warming and comforting. Then she exhaled and it wasn't until the last of the smoke had left her lungs that she coughed. She grinned as she realized she was getting the hang of it. "So what about this Marvin character. The serial killer. How do you write about a killer if you yourself haven't killed?"

"I didn't say that Marvin was the killer. Maybe he is, maybe he isn't."

"But my point stands. If all writing has to come from experience, how can you write about a serial killer?" Slater didn't reply and Jenny rolled over and looked at him. "Come on, answer the question."

He smiled easily. "This isn't an interrogation, Jenny."

"Ha! You can't answer, can you?" She grinned and lay down again. She took another pull on her cigarette. This time she inhaled and exhaled with no discomfort at all. She smiled.

Slater blew smoke. "I've killed," he said quietly.

Jenny sat up abruptly. "You have not," she said.

He nodded slowly as he stared up at the sky. "I had to," he said. "I needed to know what it felt like, to take a life."

"Bullshit," said Jenny.

Slater grinned. "Do you kiss your mother with that mouth?"

"You've killed someone? Really?"

"I didn't say I'd killed someone," said Slater. "I said that I've killed." He rolled over to face her. "Cattle," he said. "I killed cows."

Jenny frowned. "Cows?"

"I went to a slaughterhouse, in Texas. They let me kill a few. With one of those bolt gun things."

"Are you serious?"

"Sure."

"You killed cows?"

Slater mimed firing a gun. "Straight between the eyes. Bang. They're dead before they hit the ground."

"How many?"

"A dozen or so."

"And what was it like?"

Slater lay back on the grass and took another pull on his cigarette before answering. "The first time was hard," he said. "Really hard. Harder than I thought it would be. I nearly passed out and my hand was shaking like I was having an epileptic fit. I almost couldn't go through with it."

"But you did?"

"I had to. I couldn't not do it." He sighed. "The second time was easier." He chuckled. "It was like smoking. The first time was pretty horrible, the second was a bit better, and after six or seven it was fine. I could just do it. Put the gun to the cow's head and pull the trigger and bang. One dead cow. It's as easy and as complicated as that."

"Did you feel sorry? Guilty?"

Slater shrugged. "They were going to be killed no matter what I did. They were meat, pure and simple. Why should I feel guilty? I'm no guiltier than the housewife who bought the plastic-wrapped steaks at the supermarket." He pulled on his cigarette and then blew the smoke slowly through pursed lips. "But I saw what I wanted to see, Jenny. I saw living things die. I saw the life fade from their eyes and I know what it's like. I can write about it."

"And you think it's the same? Killing a cow and killing a human being?"

"Practically speaking, sure. Emotionally, no. But the book I wrote wasn't really about the emotion of killing because the killing is done by a psychopath and psychopaths don't have emotions."

"So this Marvin is a psychopath?"

Slater chuckled. "You'll have to read it."

"Come on, you can tell me. I want to know."

"I don't want to spoil it for you."

"Does he get caught?"

"Jenny…"

She reached over and tickled him in the ribs. "I want to know," she said. She held up the cigarette. "I smoked this for you," she said. "The least you can do is to tell me the plot of your novel."

"It's a novella rather than a novel," said Slater. "It's about forty thousand words, give or take. It's written from two viewpoints. There's Marvin, written in the first person. Then there's the killer, and that viewpoint's in the second person."

"So Marvin's not the killer?"

"That's the hook," said Slater. "You try to work out if both viewpoints are Marvin's, but that because he's a psychopath he thinks differently when he's in killer mode."

"And who's the hero?"

"The hero?"

"The character you identify with. Is it Marvin?"

Slater laughed. "Marvin? Hell no, Marvin's a shit. He's arrogant, he's not as smart as he thinks he is, and most of the time he has his head up his own ass."

"So who does the reader identify with?"

Slater finished his cigarette and flicked it away. "Why does the reader have to identify with anyone?"

Jenny sat up. "Are you serious?"

"It's a story. The reader doesn't have to identify with anyone."

"There are cops in it, right?"

"Sure. A man and a woman. Detectives. They're on Marvin's case. They think he's got a woman locked up somewhere and that he's torturing her before killing her."

"So they're your heroes?"

"They're pretty nasty characters too."

Jenny frowned and ran a hand through her hair. "So everyone in the book is unpleasant?"

"Pretty much."

Jenny put her head on one side and narrowed her eyes. "I don't get it."

"What's to get?"

"In a novel you have to have a protagonist that you identify with, and he or she has an obstacle that he or she has to overcome. That's what makes a story."

Slater laughed. "Is that what Grose says?"

"It's what everyone says."

Slater's eyes sparkled with amusement. "Everyone?"

"You know what I mean. Every book on creative writing says that."

"And who writes these books? Real writers write real books. The ones that write books on writing are the failed writers."

"That's a bit harsh."

"The truth often is. I wrote from the heart, Jenny. I write what I want to write, not what some failed writer thinks I should be writing." He sat up and crossed his legs. "You need to do the same," he said. He tapped his chest. "Write from the heart. Write what you believe in. Then let the readers decide."

Jenny sighed. "I wish I had your confidence."

"If you don't believe in yourself, how can you expect anyone else to?" He looked at his watch. "I've got to go." He stood up and brushed grass off the knees of his jeans, then picked up his backpack and laptop. "If you want, I'll print you off a copy of the basement story. Just promise me one thing."

"Not another cigarette?"

Slater grinned. "That was a one-off," he said. "No, just don't show it to Grose. Keep it between us. I've never shown it to anyone else and to be honest I'm pretty sure he'll hate it." He held out his hand and helped her up.

"I promise," she said. "Can you do me a favor?"

"Anything."

She laughed. "Nothing serious, I'd just prefer a PDF that's all."

Slater grinned. "Deal," he said.

"So you'll let me read it? Really?"

"You sound surprised." He unzipped one of the pockets on his backpack and took out a thumbdrive. He grinned and handed it to her. It was made from soft plastic, in the shape of a burger, complete with lettuce, tomato and a slice of cheese.

Jenny laughed as she looked at it. "You've got to be joking," she said. She pulled it apart to reveal the USB connection. "A burger?"

"It's ironic," he said. "Books are the new fast food. Cheap and disposable."

She put the thumbdrive into her pocket. "You won't really write about me in The Bestseller, will you?"

"Why? Are you scared that Dudley will read it?"

"No," she said. She shrugged. "Maybe. I don't know."

"Don't worry, you can trust me," he said. He picked up his motorcycle helmet, blew her a kiss and walked away.

Jenny watched him go. She felt a sudden craving for another cigarette and she laughed quietly to herself.

CHAPTER 10

Grose sat back in his chair, closed his eyes and groaned. The words just wouldn't come. He'd sat at his desk for the best part of two hours and all he had to show were two hundred words and he'd crossed most of them out. He just couldn't concentrate. He pushed back his chair, stood up and walked over to the window. It was dark outside and there were thick clouds obscuring the moon and stars. He looked down at the garden. There was a block of light from the kitchen illuminating part of the lawn and a shadow moved across it. His wife, probably making herself her evening cocoa. She'd had the same evening routine for the last ten years. A TV movie, usually on the Hallmark Channel with a mug of cocoa followed by half an hour in bed reading one of her insufferable romances. Grose had long given up complaining about her choice of reading matter and more often than not he stayed in his study until she was asleep.

He sat down again and picked up his pen. He sighed. He was trying to start a new novel but his mind was still buzzing with the characters in The Homecoming. The Homecoming was unfinished business, it was in limbo, trapped in a netherworld between being written and being published and he had no way of knowing how long it would remain there. The Homecoming was a good book, possibly a great book, as good as any of his earlier works. The fact that Pink hadn't wanted to sell it had come as a shock. It was the last thing that Grose had expected to hear. He knew that the sensible thing to do would be to send it out to another agent but Pink's rejection had been so hurtful that Grose couldn't bear repeating the experience. At some point he'd have to, but not just yet. He'd thought of rewriting the book, giving it another polish, but after rereading it he'd decided that there was nothing he could do to improve it. The Homecoming was perfect, and Pink was an idiot for not realizing it.

He tapped his Mont Blanc fountain pen on his notepad. He didn't have a title for the book that he was about to start writing. Generally he didn't, the titles of his books usually came to him about halfway through the writing. He had the outline of a plot. A father who discovers that his twenty-year-old son is gay and disowns him. Five years later the son is sick and needs a kidney transplant. The father offers one of his own kidneys but the son refuses. It's not a kidney he wants, it's acceptance, but the father can't give that. The book would go to the heart of what it meant to be a father, and Grose was drawing on his own experiences with his own father who had died three years earlier. It would be a moving book, powerful and emotional, but try as he could the words just wouldn't come. He wasn't even able to come up with names for the characters, and that was always a bad sign. Titles could wait, and sometimes were even changed before publication, but names were crucial. Names went to character and Grose needed a name before he could write. The father's Christian name was Gideon, Grose knew that. It was Biblical and Gideon was a man who believed in the Bible. But Grose couldn't come up with a family name and until he had that he couldn't even start to describe the man or put words in his mouth.

The opening paragraph was going to be a description of the man's house, as if the reader was approaching it from the road. It was winter and there would be a thin plume of grey smoke rising from the chimney. Grose could picture the house and the snow that covered the garden, but every time he tried to put words down onto paper they came out stilted and forced. He dropped his pen and ran his hands through his hair. It wasn't that the words wouldn't come – he had nothing but contempt for writers who claimed to be blocked – it was simply that the words that were coming were the wrong ones. The few sentences he had written would have shamed a thirteen-year-old schoolgirl.

He stood up again and paced over to the window. The block of light had gone. His wife would be in front of the TV with her feet up on the coffee table, her mug of cocoa by her side. He went over to his desk, pulled open the top drawer and took out his cell phone. He hadn't saved Jenny's number just in case his wife ever went through the phone's contacts list. He tapped out the digits from memory and held the phone to his ear as it rang out.

CHAPTER 11

Jenny jumped as her cell phone vibrated on the sofa next to her. She was curled up with her Kindle, half way through Slater's book. She had been totally immersed in the writing and stared resentfully at the vibrating phone. She had thought she'd set it to silent but clearly had once again failed to get to grips with its operating system. She picked it up and looked at the phone's screen and her heart fell when she saw who was calling. An evening call meant he was feeling lonely and needed reassurance, but also meant that he was at home with his wife.

"Dudley, hi," she said, putting down the eReader.

"God, I miss you," he said. That was the way he always started his evening calls. But if he really missed her, all he had to do was to come to her. She was the one living alone, she was the one whose door was always open. If anyone should have been doing the phoning it was her, but he'd made it clear that she was never to phone him while he was at home. It was rule number one of the Dating A Married Man game. There were a lot of rules, and over the course of the relationship she'd come to resent each and every one.

"I miss you, too," she said, but strictly speaking that wasn't true because she had been so engrossed in Slater's book that she hadn't given him a moment's thought since she'd started reading.

"What are you doing?"

"Nothing," she lied. She knew that he'd hate the fact that she was reading Slater's book. He'd see it as a betrayal, maybe even a threat, and she couldn't face an argument with him.

"Not writing?"

"I was thinking about it. I just wasn't, you know, in the mood."

"Tell me about it," he said. "I haven't written a word all day."

"Oh honey, I'm sorry. What about the agent? Have you heard back from him about The Homecoming?"

There was a long pause and she wondered if he hadn't heard her.

"Dudley? Are you there?"

"Haven't heard back from him yet," said Grose.

"The man's an idiot," said Jenny. "He should be biting your hand off."

"Or walking through walls."

"What?" Jenny picked up her Kindle with her left hand. She was keen to get back into Slater's story. She'd been gripped from the first page and she was convinced she'd just reached a major turning point. She also suspected the twist in the tail and was desperate to discover if she was right or not.

"Nothing," said Grose. He sighed. "God, I wish I was with you now."

"Come around then," she said. "I'm wearing that silk thing you like. The one with the bows on the front." That was a lie, she was wearing a NYPD sweatshirt that was several sizes too big and baggy pants that she usually wore to the gym.

"I wish I could, honey. I'd much rather be there with you."

Jenny felt a sudden rush of anger and she bit down on her lower lip to stop herself snapping at him. There were times when he acted like a spoiled child. He was a grown man, older than her father, and if he really wanted to walk out on his wife there was nothing stopping him.

"Jenny?"

She took a deep breath. "Yes, honey."

"I will leave her, I promise. I just need to get everything sorted. Once my life's in order, we'll be together."

"You swear?"

"I swear, honey."

"You need to talk to your stupid agent and get him moving on The Homecoming," she said.

"I will," he said.

Jenny found herself reading. There was something hypnotic about Slater's writing, it seemed to pull her into the story. His descriptions appeared effortless but she knew from experience how difficult it was to write well. His dialogue was amazing, she could practically hear the characters speaking as she read.

"Jenny?"

Jenny realized that he'd said something. She put down the Kindle. "Sorry, honey, it's a bad line. What did you say?"

"I said I'll see you tomorrow. And I'll come around to your place afterwards, is that okay? Spend some time together."

"Can you spend the night?"

"I'm sorry, honey. Not tomorrow. But I'll work something out. Love you."

"Love you too."

The line went dead. Jenny switched the phone to silent, tossed it onto the sofa and picked up her eReader. "God this is so good," she whispered to herself as she began to read.

CHAPTER 12

Grose adjusted the creases of his trousers and tried to keep a straight face as Stan Naghdi looked up from his laptop and took his first breath in almost three minutes. Naghdi was one of the more enthusiastic students on the course, a slim second generation Persian with slicked-back gelled hair and rat-like eyes. Naghdi blinked, flashed Grose a hopeful smile, and went back to reading from his screen. His voice was a dull, flat monotone, totally devoid of emotion. "The fighters came screaming from behind the moon, lasers blasting as they swooped down on the space station. Admiral Mackenzie screamed into his intercom. "Fire solar torpedoes!" he screamed." Stan looked up, pained. "Oh, I've used screamed twice. That's not good is it?"

"It's okay, Stan," said Grose. "Keep going."

Naghdi nodded and carried on reading. "Needle fighters burst from the space station's underbelly, breaking formation and attacking the invaders. They were heavily outnumbered, but the needle fighters were faster and harder to hit. Mackenzie watched the dog fight on the main screen. He turned to his weapons officer. "Screens down," he screamed. Oh, I've done it again." Naghdi looked up at Grose. Grose smiled and waved for him to continue. Naghdi bent down over his laptop and took another deep breath. "The weapons officer looked surprised. To drop the shields in the middle of an attack was suicide. "Just do it." Mackenzie scr....." Naghdi rubbed the back of his neck. "Yelled. He pointed at the weapons officer. "Just do it,

Sandra, I know what I'm doing. Just trust me." The weapons officer looked into Mackenzie's azure blue eyes and her lower lip trembled with passion."

Naghdi closed his laptop and looked at Grose. "That's as far as I've got."

Grose nodded thoughtfully. "It's coming on, Stan," said Grose. "Your descriptions need work, of course. And you must watch out for repetition."

"You said that last week," said a voice from the back of the room and the class laughed. It was Slater, looking over the top of his notepad, wearing his trademark RayBans.

Grose looked up at Slater, his face hardening. He wanted to ask Slater to remove his sunglasses but couldn't risk a confrontation. If Slater refused, what were his options? He could hardly force Slater to take them off.

The class gradually fell silent as they realized that Grose wasn't amused.

"Your point being what, Mr Slater?" said Grose, his voice carrying across the lecture hall.

Slater put down his notepad and stared at Grose without replying.

"Well, Mr Slater?"

Slater shrugged. "I just meant that you repeated that repetition was a bad thing, which I guess was sort of ironic. I was being funny. Or I thought I was. I guess with hindsight..." He shrugged.

Grose took off his spectacles and began to polish them. When he looked back up at Slater, all he could see was a blur. "I think it's time for you to share your work in progress with us," said Grose. "Hopefully you'll have improved it since you last gave us a reading."

"I'll pass," said Slater.

"All talk, huh?" said Grose. "Talk is cheap, Mr Slater. Anyone can talk. But being a writer takes more. It takes commitment. It takes intelligence. It takes character. To put it bluntly, it takes balls. Balls that apparently you are lacking."

Slater stared down at Grose for several seconds, then he reached into his backpack and took out a clear plastic file containing several papers. He stood up, looked around, and cleared his throat. Grose pushed his glasses high up on his head and tucked his handkerchief in his pocket.

"Chapter Two," said Slater. "The victim." He paused for effect, smiled, and then continued. "The victim is everything. The victim can't be too obscure. There'd be no challenge in picking up someone from the street, someone who'd never be missed. A prostitute would be too easy. Young and pretty would be best. Somebody's daughter. But not a child. Definitely not a child. I think that what will happen is that eventually the victim will select herself. I saw a wildlife documentary once on the National Geographic channel, about how a cheetah kills its prey. The cheetah prowls around the herd, zebras maybe, watching and waiting. The zebras can run if they want, but unless the cheetah gets too close they keep on grazing."

Pretty much all the students had twisted around in their seats to get a better look at Slater. Slater grinned, reveling in the attention, and then began to read again. "Eventually the cheetah selects its victim. It stands and stares, but still makes no move to attack. The zebra that's been chosen stands and stares back. It knows that it's going to be killed, but it doesn't run. Why? Because deep down, it wants to be killed. It wants to be a victim. Then the cheetah attacks, it breaks into the lethal sprint that ends in death, and only then does the herd scatter and the victim run. But by then it's too late. It's all over bar the killing."

Grose felt his stomach lurch as he saw that Jenny was looking up at Slater, her eyes wide, clearly enjoying the story. Jenny seemed to sense that Grose was looking at her and she turned to look at him. Their eyes locked for a couple of seconds and then Grose realized that Slater had stopped speaking. He was watching Grose with a sly smile on his face.

Slater jutted his chin forward before continuing. "I think the victim might turn out to be one of the students on this course," he said.

Grose got slowly to his feet. "That's enough, Mr Slater!" he said wearily.

Slater held out the papers he was holding. "There's more," he said. "I was up all night writing. It just seemed to flow."

"We're done, Mr Slater. I'm not having you sully this lesson with your garbage." He pointed up at Slater. "You're treading on very thin ice, very thin ice indeed. I'm this close to throwing you off this course."

Slater stared at Grose, his face impassive behind the RayBans. "Actually, I don't think you have the authority to do that, Doctor Grose."

"You don't think so?" He pointed at the door. "Out. Now."

Slater looked as if he was going to argue, but then he slowly shook his head, put his folder back into his backpack, slung it over his shoulder, picked up his motorcycle helmet and then walked down the stairs. He stopped at the door and turned to look back at Grose. "You're making a big mistake," he said.

"We'll see about that, Mr Slater," said Grose. He pointed again at the door. "Now go before I call security and have you removed."

Slater smiled, shook his head again, and pushed open the door. Grose glared after him, seething.

CHAPTER 13

Jenny walked out of the college building and was about to head for the subway when she saw Slater down the road, his long black coat flapping behind him. "Adrian!" she called, but he didn't appear to hear her and continued to stride along the sidewalk. She ran after him and caught up with him just as he was turning the corner. "Hey," she said, and then took a couple of deep breaths.

Slater grinned at her. "You're not a jogger, then," he said.

"Are you okay?"

"Sure I'm okay. Why wouldn't I be okay?"

"You got thrown off the course. How can you be so calm about it?"

Slater chuckled. "He can't do that. It's not in his power. I've paid for the course, I'm doing the work, he can't throw me off just because he doesn't like what I've written. We've got a little thing called the First Amendment, remember. He can't throw me out of an educational establishment because of something I wrote."

"He seems to think that he can."

"Yeah, well I went in to see the Dean and she's going to set him straight. To be honest, if anyone is at risk of being shown the door, it's Grose. The Dean's none too happy with him."

"You can see his point, though." She clutched her laptop bag to her chest.

Slater frowned. "You're not serious? You can see the way he's gunning for me."

"Well, you did sort of start it, making that comment about repetition."

"But he does repeat himself. Over and over again."

Jenny grinned. "Which is also repetition, isn't it?"

Slater tilted his head on one side like an inquisitive budgerigar. "What?"

"Over and over. That's repetition. It's like Pete and Re-Pete sitting on the wall."

"What the hell are you talking about?"

Jenny smiled. "Pete and Re-Pete are sitting on a wall. Pete falls off. So now who's sitting on the wall?"

"Re-Pete."

"Okay. Pete and Re-Pete are sitting on a wall. Pete falls off. So now who's sitting on the wall?"

"Re-Pete."

"Okay. Pete and Re-Pete are sitting…"

Slater laughed and held up his hand. "I get it," he said. "How old are you? Ten?" He nodded at her laptop bag. "So what did you think of The Basement?"

"How do you know it's in my bag?"

Slater smiled. "I saw you reading it at lunch. I was going to go over but you seemed so engrossed that I left you to it."

Jenny patted her bag. "Can we go for coffee?"

"That sounds ominous. Are you breaking up with me?"

Her mouth opened in surprise and then she realized that he was joking. "I'll buy," she said. "You got them last time."

They walked together to Starbucks and this time Slater grabbed a table while Jenny fetched the coffees. She frowned as she stirred sugar into her coffee. "Can I be honest with you?" she asked.

"You can be frank."

"Frank?"

"It's sort of a joke. You say "Can I be frank" and I say "You can be whoever the hell you want" and we both laugh."

"But I asked if I could be honest."

"I was rewriting your dialogue as we went along. It's a thing I do. In my head."

Jenny finished stirring her coffee and put down the spoon. "Sometimes I can't tell if you're being serious or not."

"Generally not," said Slater. "But go on. You can be Frank. Or Ernest."

"Honest," she said, opening her bag and taking out the thumdrive he'd given her. "I'll be honest." She pushed it across the table towards him. "I might say something that you don't want to hear."

"Oh dear."

"I don't mean that it's not well written. It's brilliantly written. It grabbed me from the first page and I read it in one sitting." She sat back in her chair. "It's a fast read, lots of pace, and the dialogue is perfect. I really could hear their voices."

Slater smiled. "There's a "but" coming, isn't there?"

She nodded. "It was just..." She shrugged. "I don't know what the word is. Bleak? Soulless? It has no heart."

"No heart?"

"No one in it has any redeeming features. I think that's because really there are only three characters of any weight – Marvin and the two cops. And you can't empathize with any of them."

"Why do you need to empathise?"

"Because you have to be rooting for someone. And you've no real sympathy for the woman in the basement because you never really get to know her. She's just a victim. But because you don't care for her, there's no ticking clock, no race against time to save her." She frowned. "You're not annoyed are you?"

Slater smiled easily. "Of course not. I wanted your honest opinion."

"I'm sorry."

"Sorry? Why?"

"Because I'm not saying it's the greatest book I've ever read. Because I'm picking it apart." She smiled sympathetically. "You don't mind me being critical, do you?"

"I want honesty," said Slater. "If you hate it you hate it. I'd rather you look me in the eyes and say that than pretend you love it just so as not to hurt my feelings."

"Don't get me wrong, I didn't hate it. I found it fascinating, and the writing was great. It really flowed. It was hard to put down, it was as if you were dragging me through the story by the scruff of the neck."

Slater smiled, obviously pleased.

"The problem is like I said, you don't empathize with anyone. And there's no happy ending."

Slater chuckled. "That's life, Jenny. Any story that ends with a happy ending hasn't really ended. It's like when Snow White rides off into the sunset with Prince Charming, you know it's not really going to end happily ever after, the chances are that before long she'll put on weight and he'll be off having affairs with Cinderella and Sleeping Beauty. There are no happy endings in the real world, Jenny. You know that."

"You are the cynic, aren't you? The thing is, if you don't have a sympathetic character then you don't know who to root for."

"So you're saying you need the writer to tell you who the hero is? I don't agree." Slater picked up the thumbdrive and put it into his backpack. "I didn't want any of the characters to be sympathetic," he said. "That's not what I was trying to do. I wanted to see if I could write a book in two viewpoints, one in the first person and one in the second person."

"That worked brilliantly," she said.

"And then I wanted the big twist at the end, which calls into question everything that you've read up to that point."

"And that worked too," she said. "I never saw the twist coming. But I'm not sure that the average reader is going to like the fact that there's no one to empathize with. Have you shown it to an agent?"

Slater shook his head. "There's no point. You're right, it doesn't fit the mold of what sells. And it's too short. It's not long enough to be a stand-alone book. I mean what would it be at best, a hundred pages? A hundred and twenty? Who publishes books that long? No one."

"So what was the point of writing it? Was it an exercise?" She picked up her coffee and sipped it.

"I'm going to publish it myself," he said. "I don't think a traditional publisher will touch it. So I'll do it myself."

"That's a good idea," she said. "John Grisham self-published A Time To Kill and look what happened to him."

"John who?" asked Slater. Jenny was about to answer when she realized that he was joking and she put a hand up to cover her mouth. "But only when the time is right," he said. "I want to finish the book I'm working on now. That's going to be the big one. My break-out book. I'll publish The Basement on the back of it." He sipped his coffee, then wiped foam from his upper lip with the back of his hand. "So tell me about your book. The romance. How's it going?"

"Slowly," she said.

"You've finished the first chapter?"

"I'm not happy with it but I've moved on. Dudley says I..." She stopped herself but it was too late, Slater was already grinning at her. "Don't look at me like that," she said. "He's read it and he was offering me some advice."

"So you won't tell me about your work but you'll show him?"

"He's running the course, Adrian. He's going to be marking me."

Slater chuckled. "This course isn't about marks. It's about producing a book. At the end of the day it's the books that we write that matter, not what marks Grose gives us."

"I need the marks towards my degree," said Jenny. "Don't you?"

"I don't give a shit about a degree," he said. "I just want to write a book that'll sell a million copies."

Jenny laughed. "Come on, Adrian."

"I'm serious," he said, staring at her intently. "Education doesn't count for anything anymore. All you need these days is a laptop and Google and you've got access to all the knowledge in the world, pretty much. And you think a reader cares if the writer of the book they've just downloaded has a degree or a PhD or if they even finished High School?"

"Downloaded?" repeated Jenny. "You're talking eBooks. Not real books?"

"There's no difference. A book is a book is a book. What matters is how many people read that. Actually, cancel that. What matters is how many people PAY to read a book."

"So you don't care if your work is published or not?"

"EBooks are published. All published really means is being offered for sale. I don't care who buys my book or how they buy it so long as I get their money."

Jenny grinned. "So you're a mercenary, a cynic and a rebel?"

"I am truly multi-talented, yes." He put his head on one side as he looked at her. "I know what I want, Jenny, and I know how to get what I want. Sometimes that scares people. It's a wolf and sheep thing."

"You're a wolf, is that it? And everyone else is a sheep?"

"Not everyone, no. But there are more sheep than wolves out there, and they always get nervous when they know that there's a wolf around."

"And what am I, Adrian? Sheep or wolf?"

"Don't you know?"

"I'm more interested in what you think I am."

Slater narrowed his eyes as he sipped his coffee. "You're not a sheep, Jenny. If you were, you wouldn't be here with me."

"So I'm a wolf?"

He put down his cup and grinned. "Let's just say you've got wolfish tendencies," he said.

"What does that mean? I'm a wolf in sheep's clothing?"

"More like the reverse. You're a sheep in transition."

"I'm not sure if I should be offended or not."

Slater laughed. He looked so much more handsome when he laughed, Jenny realized. More often than not in class he had a slight frown, as if something was troubling him, and usually there was a blank look to his eyes as if his mind was somewhere else, but sitting opposite her in the coffee shop he was totally focused on her and so much more relaxed. Without his trademark RayBans she could see that his eyes were a deep blue and had a girl's lashes, long and black. His skin was so smooth that she kept having to fight the urge to reach out and stroke his cheek. "I really would like to read your work, Jenny," he said. "I can tell from talking to you that you've got talent."

"You're just saying that," she said.

Slater shook his head. "I'm not like that. I don't lie. Life's too short."

Jenny sighed. "I don't know," she said.

"You don't know what?"

"If I want someone to read what I've written. You might hate it."

"But if I did, I'd tell you why I'd hate it and I'd probably tell you how to improve it. How's that a bad thing?"

"It's not, I suppose."

"Exactly. But I can promise you one thing, you'll get an honest opinion, and that's more than you'll get from Grose."

"Dudley's honest with me, he always has been," said Jenny, quickly. Too quickly, she realized, and her hand went up to cover her mouth.

"He wants to get inside your pants, Jenny. You must know that. And you must know he's married."

"Why are you so mean?" she asked.

"I'm honest. I tell it like it is. He's a fifty-one year old man who hasn't written anything of any substance for almost twenty-five years. You've heard the old saying, right? "Those that can, do. Those that can't, teach'. That's exactly where Grose is. He wrote a couple of decent books when he was younger but for whatever reason he hasn't been able to repeat it. So now he teaches. Which means that we're being taught by a writer who can't write, which when you think about it is a pretty pointless exercise."

"So why did you enroll on the course?"

Slater shrugged carelessly. "I wanted to spend some time in New York. I wrote The Basement while I was in LA and I wanted to check that I'd captured the city. And I wanted to get feedback. That's about the only good thing about the course, the fact that we get to critique each other's work. So, will you show me your work in progress?"

"You'll be gentle with me?"

"I'll be honest," he said. "And if I hate it I'll be honest and gentle."

Jenny reached into her laptop bag. There were several small pouches on the inside and in one of them was a small green thumbdrive. She took it out and slid it across the table to him.

"Don't forget my burger," he said.

"Burger?"

"The burger with The Basement on it."

"Sorry," said Jenny. She fumbled in her bag, found the thumbdrive and gave it to him.

"What are you doing this evening?" he asked.

"Why?" She realized she was sounding defensive and she forced a smile.

"I was going to offer to take you for a drink, that's all."

"Rain check," she said. "I've got to get some writing done."

"Haven't we all?" said Slater. "I'll hold you to that rain check."

CHAPTER 14

The Head of Faculty sneered at Grose as if he'd just broken wind. "Dudley, I really don't see what the problem is."

Her name was Belinda Kellaway though she preferred to be called Linda. She was in her early thirties, overweight but dressed to hide it, favoring long shirts over long dresses and baggy jackets with the sleeves turned up. She wore little or no makeup and clear varnish on her nails. Behind her on the wall were her framed credentials and degrees. There were a lot of them.

"The problem is that Adrian Slater is threatening to kill a fellow student," said Grose. "Haven't I made that clear?"

"Mr Slater is a student on your creative writing course and he was reading from his work in progress, that's what you said."

"Yes, and he said that he was going to choose a victim from among the students on the course." He sighed and shook his head. "I don't think I can make myself any clearer."

"But it's a novel, you said."

"No, I said it was supposed to be a novel. But he's working on something called The Bestseller which he says involves him killing a fellow student and writing about it."

Kellaway chuckled dryly. "Dudley, if he was really going to commit murder, he'd hardly stand up and announce the fact to the world."

"Unless he's a psychopath and doesn't care."

"Is that what you think? You're not a psychiatrist, are you?"

"Of course I'm not a psychiatrist. But that's not the point. The point is that he's talking about killing a student and I'm not prepared to have him in my class. He's off the course."

Kellaway looked pained. "I'm not sure that we can do that, Dudley. We can't go throwing students off courses just because their lecturer doesn't agree with their views."

"Views? Who said anything about views?" Grose wanted to stand up but he knew that she'd see that as aggression so he took a deep breath and forced himself to relax. "He stood up in front of the class and said he was going to kill to write a bestseller."

"It's an expression, Dudley. Probably every writer in the world has said that at one time or another."

"Today he started talking about zebras and cheetahs and the jungle and then he said that he was thinking about targeting a student. A student, Linda. How do you think it's going to look if a student dies and the Media finds out that we knew about this?"

"But that's not going to happen," she said. "Seriously, Dudley, what is your issue with this Adrian Slater? It can't be just about the book. There has to be more to it than that."

Grose threw up his hands in frustration. He wanted to snap at the stupid woman and tell her what he really thought of her, but he knew that would achieve nothing. Kellaway simply wasn't listening to him.

"Dudley, I'm not sure that now is a good time for you to be picking fights with one of your students. Not with the way things are?"

"What do you mean?"

She flashed him a tight smile as if he was her cleaner and she'd just asked him to give the stove a going over. "There's talk of revamping the course, and perhaps bringing in a younger teaching staff."

"What? What do you mean there's talk? Who's talking?"

"I'm not in a position to say."

"You're the Head of Faculty, Linda. You must know."

"I didn't say that I didn't know, Dudley. I said that I wasn't in a position to say. But just be aware that there are those who'd like to go with a younger structure and that changes could be made to the curriculum to make it more modern."

"Modern? In what way." He leaned forward. "You're talking about letting me go? Is that what you're saying?"

"Of course not, Dudley. No one is even suggesting that, not at the moment anyway. But the world of publishing is changing and perhaps the courses we are offering need to change along with it. Perhaps we should be looking forward and not back."

Grose frowned, not understanding what she was getting at.

Kellaway smiled at his confusion. "EBooks are the way forward, Dudley. EPublishing is the future. We should be teaching our students how to write eBooks, and how to market and promote them. We should be showing them how to get their work out into the marketplace and communicating directly with their readers."

Grose's eyes widened with horror. He felt as if he'd just been punched in the stomach. He knew exactly what the Head of Faculty was planning. A new industry, a new course, and if the existing lecturers weren't up to the job, then a new teaching staff.

"You see what I mean, Dudley. Our courses are becoming more user-led, rather than dictating to our students we need to be more open to their needs and wants, we must start helping them develop their talents rather than pushing them to conform to what our idea of success is."

Grose nodded despondently, then forced a smile. "Absolutely," he said. "Amazing technology." He stood up. "Well, thanks for your time anyway, Linda."

"A pleasure, Dudley." She was already looking at her computer screen. "My door is always open."

CHAPTER 15

Jenny dipped her wooden spoon into the bolognaise sauce and tentatively touched her tongue to it. She decided it needed a bit more salt and added some, just as her buzzer sounded. She pressed the button to let Grose in and stirred her sauce as she waited for him to come up to her floor. He tapped on the front door and she opened it and kissed him at the threshold.

"Something smells good," he said.

"Is it me or the food?" she asked.

"Both," he said. He walked over to the sofa and tossed his briefcase onto her armchair as he sat down heavily.

"Bad day?" she asked.

"Faculty meeting," he said. "It just went on and on." He looked at his wristwatch. "I'm going to have to be out of here by ten," he said.

Jenny tried not to show her disappointment but he wasn't even looking at her. He reached for her eReader and switched it on. "I can't believe you read on a thing like this," he said.

"Dudley, it's brilliant," she said. "I can put three thousand books on it," she said. "Do you know how much space three thousand books would take up?"

"One good book is worth three thousand bad ones," said Grose. "This is just a glorified calculator."

She put a handful of spaghetti into a pot of boiling salted water. "The battery lasts for weeks and I can buy any book I want within seconds," she said. "It's like having the biggest library in the world at my fingertips."

Grose snorted. "You sound like a salesman," he said.

"I'm a convert."

"A zealot."

"Dudley, really, you should try it. Once you've tried an eReader it's hard to go back to dead tree books."

Grose raised his eyebrows. "What did you say? Dead tree books?"

"It's what they call paperbacks these days. Think of all the trees that can be saved if everybody read eBooks? Think of the energy that's wasted making books, all the water that's wasted in making paper." She took two plates out of a cupboard and put them next to the stove.

"First of all pretty much all paper is made from sustainable timber," said Grose. "For every tree that's cut down, the companies plant another two. And pretty much all the water that's used is recycled." He sighed. "Why am I even discussing this with you? It's not about the environment or energy conservation, it's about books. Books are meant to be held, the pages turned with reverence not by pushing a button. Reading is a tactile pleasure as well as stimulation for the intellect. You might as well read a novel on a laptop."

"It's almost the same as a dead..." She stopped herself. "As a real book," she said. "There's no backlight so it feels like you're reading a page rather than a screen. It's better for your eyes, they say. And there's no glare so you can read it outside no matter what the light."

Grose chuckled. "You really are sounding like a salesman now," he said.

"Red or white?" she said.

"What?" he said, confused by the change of subject.

"Wine." she said. "I've got a Pinot Grigio in the fridge."

"That'll be fine," he said as he studied the screen. "So what are you reading?"

"Nothing," she said as she opened the fridge.

He looked at her over the top of his glasses. "Nothing?" he repeated. "You spent what, a hundred bucks, on it and you read nothing?"

"I meant nothing important," she said. She uncorked the wine, poured some into two glasses and took them over to Grose. He took one of the glasses and she reached for the cReader. He moved it out of her reach. "Dudley, please…"

Grose looked back at the screen. "Nothing?" he said. He pressed a button and the screen was filled with words.

"Dudley," Jenny pleaded. "Give it to me."

"What is this?" he said. "It reads like some awful pulp fiction story."

"It's nothing. Come on, put it down. We don't have much time left."

She tried to grab the Kindle but Grose turned his back to her. His face hardened as he finished reading what was on the screen and pressed the button to get the next page.

"What is this?"

"It's nothing."

"The Basement. By Adrian Slater." He looked at her, his face as hard as stone.

"Dudley…"

He turned to look at her and held up the eReader. "What the hell is his book doing on here? Did you buy it?"

"It's not for sale. It's not published yet."

"So how did it get on this thing?"

"It's not a thing, Dudley. It's a Kindle. My Kindle." She held out her hand. "Please give it to me."

"How did an unpublished book get on here?"

"He gave it to me on a thumbdrive."

"But why? Why did he give it to you?"

"He wanted a second opinion. Please, Dudley, let me have it. Supper's ready."

Grose continued to stare at the screen. "That's what the course is for," he said. "For feedback. Peer review." He looked across at Jenny. "Is there something going on between the two of you?"

"Dudley, that's crazy," protested Jenny.

"Is it? I've seen him looking at you in class."

"For God's sake, Dudley, we're students on the same course. Of course he's going to look at me."

Grose waved the Kindle at her. "And how many students did he give his book to? Because Slater doesn't seem like the sharing type."

"Dudley, he just wanted a second opinion. That's all." She sat down next to him and rubbed his leg, just above the knee. "Please, let's not fight."

"This isn't a fight," said Grose, looking at her over the top of his spectacles. "I'm just trying to ascertain what's going on."

Jenny sighed. "Honey, nothing's going on."

"So what do you think?" asked Grose.

"About what?"

"About what he's written. His book."

She shrugged. "I haven't finished it yet."

"What about what you've read so far?"

"It's interesting," she said. "But it's hard to identify with any of the characters. It's very plot driven."

"But you're enjoying it?"

Jenny screwed up her face, not sure what to say. She knew that Grose had taken a dislike to Adrian but she didn't want to lie to him and tell him how much she was enjoying the story. It was gritty and edgy, and she'd never read anything like it. "It's very easy to read," she said. "It flows. And the dialogue is really good."

"So the answer is yes, you are enjoying it." He gave it to her and she stood up and took it over to her desk, afraid that he would take it from her again. He had a temper at times and she could imagine him hurling it against the wall. "I still don't understand why he gave it to you to read."

"I think he was just worried that people might laugh at it," she lied. "He wanted to know if it was good enough to read out in class, that's all." She didn't like having to lie to him, but she could see that he was spoiling for an argument.

"What about this piece of crap he's working on now. That Bestseller nonsense."

"What do you mean?"

"Has he given you that to read?"

She shook her head. "No."

"Have you talked to him about it?" He studied her over the top of his wineglass.

"No. Not really."

Grose smiled. "I've spoken to the police about him."

"You've what? Dudley, why would you do that?"

"He's talking about killing a student. He can't get away with that."

Jenny put her eReader into the top drawer of the desk and went to sit down next to Grose. "The protagonist is. But that's not Adrian. I mean it is his voice, but it's not actually him. He's playing a role. He's pretending to be a killer. Remember American Psycho? Bret Easton Ellis?"

"I know who wrote American Psycho, Jenny," said Grose primly.

"Yes, but no one thought that Ellis was Patrick Bateman, did they? No one ever accused Ellis of being a serial killer."

"But Ellis was writing about fictional characters. Slater isn't."

"Which is why his book is so edgy."

"Edgy? Is that what you think?"

"I haven't read it, Dudley. All I know about it is what he read out in class."

He looked at her slyly. "Will you do something for me, honey?"

She didn't like the tone of his voice. It was as if he was humoring her, treating her like a child. It was the tone her mother had used when she wanted Jenny to tidy her room or wash the dishes. "What?"

"Ask Slater if he'll let you have a copy of his work in progress."

"He won't do that. Why would he do that?"

"He gave you one of his books to read. Why wouldn't he give you what he's working on?"

"I don't like this, Dudley."

Grose pointed a finger at her face. "I knew there was something going on," he said.

"Don't be ridiculous."

"If there was nothing going on you wouldn't have a problem with me reading it. It's my course, Jenny. I'll be marking his work eventually so I'm going to have to read it at some point." He sighed. "I'm very disappointed in you. I thought you trusted me."

"I do, Dudley!" she said.

"Clearly you don't," he said.

"Dudley!" she protested. "You're being horrible."

"I just don't see why you won't help me," said Grose. He looked at his watch.

"Please, honey. Let's not fight. Okay, I'll try to get a copy. Okay? Are you happy now?"

He stroked her face. "Don't get mad," he said.

"I'm not mad. But it's like you don't trust me."

"I trust you honey," he said. "Of course I do." He leaned over and kissed her on the lips.

She kissed him back, hard, and he slipped a hand up to cup her breast. "Let's go to bed," he said.

"Supper's ready," she said.

"Bed first," he said. "Supper can wait."

CHAPTER 16

Slater lit a cigarette and blew smoke over the top of his laptop, then began to type. The words came quickly and he had to make a conscious effort to slow himself down because the faster he typed the more mistakes he made. Writing had always come easily to Slater. He was able to picture a scene in his mind, movie-like, and then transfer that to a written description with next to no effort. He was rarely lost for a word and only occasionally did he have to resort to using a thesaurus. There were two books next to his laptop, a Collins dictionary and a Roget's thesaurus, both well-thumbed because he'd had them for more than ten years. They were a Christmas gift from his mother, and she'd signed them both, "To Adrian, With Love For Ever. And Ever And Ever And Ever And Ever And Ever." She'd had her third nervous breakdown just six months after giving him the books.

As he pecked away at the keyboard he heard soft footsteps on the pier and hushed voices. A man and a woman. He carried on typing, bending low over the keyboard as he worked. Something metallic tapped against the porthole behind him and he sighed and sat back in his chair. He ran his hands through his hair. It had taken him the best part of an hour to get into the zone, the place where the words came thick and fast, and now the spell was broken. He turned around. There was a man peering through the glass, holding up a detective's shield. "Mr Slater?"

"Who wants to know?" asked Slater.

The detective waved his badge. "New York Police Department," he said.

"I know, I was being ironic," said Slater.

"Can we have a few words with you, Mr Slater?"

"How about filigree, octopus and snowflake?"

The detective frowned. "What?"

"You wanted a few words, there they are. You have a nice day." Slater turned around and looked at his laptop screen. Slater knew that the detective wouldn't go away, he was just messing with him. He smiled as the detective tapped on the porthole with his badge again. Slater turned around. "Now what?"

"We'd like a conversation, Mr Slater. Face to face. Can we come aboard?"

Slater pushed himself out of his chair and walked to the rear of the cabin and pulled back the hatch. He climbed up the stairs. It had been dark for a few hours but the marina's lights were on. One of them was shining directly down onto his yacht and he shaded his eyes with the flat of his hand as he struggled to focus.

The detective who'd knocked on the porthole was in his late forties with graying swept-back hair and the look of a bloodhound whose best years were behind it – tired, watery eyes, broken blood vessels in his cheeks and heavy jowls. He showed his badge to Slater. "My name is Sergeant Mitchell," he said. "Ed Mitchell. My colleague is Joe Lumley."

Lumley was a decade younger, a few inches taller and a lot more feminine but she had the same world-weary eyes as if she'd long since given up hope of anyone ever telling her the truth. Her hair was sun-bleached blonde, cut shoulder-length, and she had a deep tan as if she spent a lot of time outdoors. She smiled showing gleaming white teeth and held out her badge.

"Short for Joanne?" asked Slater.

She smiled amiably as if she'd been asked the question a thousand times. "My dad wanted a boy," she said. "Joe's what it says on my birth certificate." She put her badge away. She was wearing a charcoal grey suit over a pale blue polo-neck and as she slid the badge into an inside pocket he caught a glimpse of a large automatic nestled in a nylon shoulder holster.

"I thought detectives mostly kept their guns on their belts," said Slater.

"We're flexible," said Lumley. "I find the belt holster ruins the line of the suit."

"Good to know," said Slater.

"Why?" asked Lumley. "Why's that good to know?"

"I'm a writer," said Slater. "Details like that, it helps with authenticity."

"Can we come aboard and have a talk?" asked Mitchell.

"Do you have business cards?" asked Slater.

"Business cards?" repeated Mitchell.

"Yeah, cards with your names and stations and phone numbers and stuff. I always prefer business cards to badges. You give them out to contacts, witnesses, snitches."

Mitchell smiled thinly, took out his wallet and gave Slater a card. Slater looked at it, then nodded at Lumley. "Can I have yours as well?"

Lumley looked across at Mitchell and the sergeant nodded. Lumley took a card from her wallet and gave it to Slater, her face a blank mask. The amiable smile had vanished along with the badge. Slater smiled brightly and slipped the cards into the back pocket of his jeans. "So how can I help New York's finest?"

"Can we come aboard?" asked Mitchell.

"Do you have a warrant?"

"We just want a chat, Mr Slater. There's no need for a warrant."

"You don't have anything to hide do you, Mr Slater?" asked Lumley.

Slater turned to look at the younger detective. The suit was expensive, the polo-neck looked as if it was cashmere and the shoes were Prada. There was a slim gold watch on her left wrist and the belt looked Italian. Slater doubted that she could afford clothes and shoes like that on a detective's salary and the woman had the arrogance of an Ivy League education. "Did you go to Columbia, detective?" he asked.

Lumley frowned. "Yes," she said hesitantly.

"Law?"

"Do we know each other?" asked Lumley.

"Just an educated guess," said Slater. "Law is just about the only subject that would lead to a career in law enforcement and Columbia is local. But assuming you graduated then you'd know that it's just not in my best interests to allow you onto my boat unless you've got a warrant. Suppose there was a body down there. If I let you on board and you see the body then I'm in trouble."

"Do you have a body in there, Mr Slater?" asked the sergeant.

"It doesn't have to be a body," said Slater. "It could just as relevantly be a dozen illegal immigrants or a kilo of Colombia's finest. My point is that I gain absolutely nothing by allowing you into my personal space."

"Do you have something down there that you don't want us to see, Mr Slater?" asked Mitchell.

"Now you're fishing, Sergeant," said Slater.

"We could come back with a warrant," said Lumley.

Slater shrugged carelessly. "You could try, but I doubt that a judge is going to grant you a warrant just because you think there's a body down there. He's going to want to know what evidence you have."

"There's the book that you're writing."

"And you have copy of that, do you?" He grinned when he saw the look of annoyance on the detective's face. "Of course you don't. So what other evidence do you have that might persuade a judge to give you a warrant. The fact that you don't like the cut of my jib?"

"The what?"

"The cut of my jib. It's a nautical expression. And the cut of my jib is no reason for a judge to sign a warrant for you to go searching through my home. And that's what this boat is. My home."

"It's the book that we want to talk about, Mr Slater," said Mitchell. Sweat was beading on his forehead and he wiped it with his sleeve. "The university is concerned that…"

"The university?" interrupted Slater. "A university is an inanimate institution. It isn't capable of thought or concern."

"Doctor Grose. The lecturer in charge of the creative writing course. He's told us about the book that you're writing."

"And?

"And like Doctor Grose, we're also concerned.

"It's the grammar, right?" said Slater.

Mitchell frowned. "The grammar?"

"Yeah, it's my grammar that lets me down. And the descriptive passages aren't as good as they might be."

"It's not the grammar that concerns us," said the sergeant. "It's the content."

"Content?"

"He's messing with us," said Lumley, reaching for the handcuffs she had in a pouch on her belt. "He can talk to us downtown."

"Are you going to arrest me, Detective Lumley? Because you'll need probable cause and I don't see that you've got that. What do you think, Sergeant Mitchell? A wrongful arrest suit isn't going to look good on your record, is it?"

Mitchell looked over at Lumley and gave her a small shake of the head. Lumley let go of her handcuffs.

"Here's the thing, Mr Slater. Doctor Grose is concerned that your book is some sort of blueprint. For a murder."

Slater laughed. "It's a novel. A work of fiction."

"About killing a student."

Slater shook his head. "It's a book, sergeant. A book about a serial killer. But just because it's written in the first person doesn't mean that I'm a killer."

"So what was that about having a body in the boat?" asked Lumley.

"That was me messing with you, detective. For which I apologize. It's just my sense of humor." He shrugged. "I'm a writer. Sometimes I play around with dialogue, just to see what effect it has."

"You need to be careful with that, Mr Slater," said Lumley. "You could end up in trouble."

"I'll be sure to bear that in mind, Detective Lumley. The last thing I want is trouble with New York's finest." His smile widened. "Can I ask you a question?"

"Depends on what it is."

"Who was it who decided that Courtesy, Respect and Professionalism was a sensible slogan to promote the NYPD."

"Why?" asked Lumley.

"Because it spells CRAP. Why would they want police officers driving around with CRAP on their vehicles. Isn't that weird?"

"It's Courtesy, Professionalism and Respect," said Mitchell.

"Really?" Slater nodded. "Well, you live and learn."

"Do you have a driver's license, Mr Slater?" asked Mitchell.

"Why would I drive in New York?"

"I didn't ask if you drove, I asked if you had a driver's license."

"Because you want to know my date of birth. So you can run a check on me. It's the one thing that never changes, but you know that of course. Your weight can go up and down, you can dye your hair, you can wear contacts, but your date of birth is the one constant that follows you throughout your life. Which is why it's the lynchpin of any database."

"So what is it, Mr Slater? Your date of birth?"

"I don't have to tell you, sergeant. So I'm not going to."

"We can get it from the university," said Lumley.

"Then do that," said Slater.

"You're not being very cooperative," said the sergeant.

"Why should I be?" asked Slater. "I'm on a creative course and the idiot who's running the course takes a dislike to the book and calls in the cops. Whatever happened to my First Amendment rights."

"This isn't about your right to Free Speech," said Mitchell. "It's about you threatening to kill a fellow student."

"It's a book," said Slater. "A novel. A work of fiction."

"In which you threaten to kill a student on the course," said Mitchell, folding his arms.

"And you know that, how?" asked Slater.

"What do you mean?"

"Have you read a copy? Because if you have, I'd be interested to know how you got hold of it."

Mitchell looked uncomfortable but didn't reply.

"So I guess you haven't got a copy," said Slater.

"You read out an excerpt in class," said Lumley.

"Which was then reported to you second-hand by Doctor Grose," said Slater. "Which makes it hearsay."

"Have you studied law, Mr Slater?" asked Lumley.

"Would you treat me with more respect if I had, Miss Lumley?"

"You can't go around threatening people, Mr Slater."

"I didn't. I read a few words from my work in progress."

"About killing a student," said Mitchell.

"It was hypothetical. What might be. Dozens of crime writers write books from the point of view of serial killers, there's nothing new in that. What about Thomas Harris? Are you going to arrest him for getting inside the head of Hannibal Lecter?"

"If he threatened to kill someone, yes," said Mitchell.

"I didn't threaten to kill anybody," said Slater. He looked at his watch. "Look, it's getting late and I want to finish the chapter I'm on."

"How about letting us have a copy of your novel, Mr Slater?" asked Lumley. "So that we can put our minds at rest?"

"I don't think so," said Slater.

"We could get a warrant," said Lumley.

"And good luck with that," said Slater. "You come back when you've got one."

He turned to go back down below deck.

"Just one more thing, Mr Slater," said Mitchell. "We'll be watching you from now on. You make one false move and we'll be coming down on you like…"

"A ton of bricks?" Slater finished for him.

"Don't play the smart mouth with me, Slater," said Mitchell.

"And don't you play the hard cop with me, Sergeant," said Slater. "Just show me the courtesy, respect and professionalism that you are supposed to and we'll get along just fine."

He turned his back on the detectives and went down the stairs into the main cabin. He lit a cigarette and watched through one of the portholes as they walked together down the pier. "Arse clowns," he muttered to himself, then sat down in front of his laptop and began to type.

CHAPTER 17

Grose sat back in his chair and tried to keep a polite smile on his face as Vicki Callas continued to drone on in her dull monotone voice. It was the second time she'd read from her work in progress and he knew from experience that she didn't take criticism well. She was in her mid-fifties but looked older, her hair graying and her breasts sagging and her skin damaged by too much time in the sun. Callas was a former prostitute turned madam turned wannabe writer though Grose doubted that anyone in his right mind would ever have paid her for sex. Frankly he doubted that anyone would ever pay for a book of hers either.

Callas had been quite open about her former profession, and even had a website which she used to offer advice to women who wanted to work in the escort business. And when she had offered to do the first reading she had spent the first five minutes explaining that she was writing from the heart because her novel about a call girl working in Fort Lauderdale was based on her own experiences.

Grose didn't know what the woman had been like as a prostitute, but her writing was dull, flat and tedious, with an undercurrent of bitterness towards men. He figured she probably exhibited the same characteristics in bed.

After the first reading he had suggested that she tone down her protagonist's hatred of men so that she'd become a more sympathetic character but she had launched a tirade of accusations: that he was a typical male, that he had no understanding of what it was like to be a downtrodden

woman in a male-dominated world, that it was because of men that she had
been forced to sell her body, that all men were abusers and rapists and that
as far as she was concerned to attack her work was to attack her as a female.
Grose had managed to calm her down but he'd learned his lesson. Callas
was unhinged and would benefit from a course of Prozac but he couldn't
take the risk of her bursting into the Dean's office and accusing him of
sexism so he just sat and smiled and nodded.

"The man opened his wallet and pulled out a handful of bills. He held
them out to Debbie, his trembling hand bathed in sweat. "On the dresser,"
she said. "Don't you know that you never hand over the money. And put it
in an envelope. The man frowned. She could see that he was nervous.
Nervous and stupid. He'd been wearing a wedding ring but he'd taken it
off and she could see the pale skin at the base of the finger. Why did he
think that she'd care about whether or not he was married?

"The man swallowed nervously. "I don't have an envelope," he said.
She pointed at the desk by the door. "Use the hotel stationery." The man
waddled over to the desk and picked up the envelope. "Two hundred and
fifty, right?" Debbie glared at the man with cold eyes. "If you mention
money again I'm out of here," she said. "We don't discuss money. You
don't hand me the money. Those are the rules." The man apologized like
the wimp he was, put the bills in the envelope and put the envelope on the
dresser. "Now what?" he said.

"Debbie pointed at the bathroom. "You shower. Everywhere. And
clean your teeth." The man nodded enthusiastically, like a little boy about
to enter a sweet shop. "Will you kiss me?" he asked. "On the mouth?"
Debbie sighed. "Of course not." She pointed at the bathroom door. "The
clock's ticking." The man waddled into the bathroom and after a few
seconds Debbie heard the shower kick into life. She took off her coat. She
wasn't wearing a dress, just a matching red bra and panties, black stockings
and suspenders. She lay down on the bed and looked at her watch. Ten
minutes gone, fifty to go. Then she had to get to Rite-Aid to pick up her

Zivorax and then get home in time to meet her daughter off the school bus. The babysitter was coming at seven and she had her third appointment of the day at the Marriott Hotel at eight. Three hours. He was a regular, flying in from Chicago, and he was a good payer. The agreed fee was a thousand but he always gave her a tip on top. He was one of her best-looking clients, tall and well-groomed and he knew not to take liberties, like trying to kiss her on the lips or trying to get her to screw without a condom. Debbie never kissed. Ever. And she never let the client go bareback, even a guy like the Chicago client who was married and had never had an STD in his entire life. The shower stopped running and Debbie took a deep breath, preparing herself for what was to come."

Callas looked up from her laptop. "That's as far as I've got," she said.

"Well done, Vicki," said Grose. "It's really coming along well." He looked around the lecture hall, deliberately avoiding eye contact with Jenny. "What does everyone else think?"

Half a dozen of the students raised their hands and Grose went to them from left to right. All six were complimentary and none expressed any reservations about the subject matter. Grose knew that they were scared of retaliation down the line, that if they criticized Callas she'd be gunning for them with both barrels when it was their turn to read. The longer the course went on the more Grose realized that what he was doing was basically pointless. He wasn't allowed to make the course competitive and there was no real attempt made to criticize bad and mediocre work. How was anyone expected to improve their craft if all they ever heard was how wonderful their work was?

Grose was a big fan of the ten thousand hours theory, that no matter what the skill or the craft that was how long it took to acquire it. It went for mastering a musical instrument, learning a foreign language, painting, even learning a trade like plumbing or carpentry. To master the skill you had to put in the hours, you had to pay your dues. And that went for writing, too. You could pretty much throw away everything you wrote during those first ten thousand hours, it was a rite of passage that every writer had to go through, in the way that artists made dozens of sketches before finally picking up a paintbrush and starting work on their masterpiece. Grose had certainly put in the hours while he was in his twenties. He'd written six novels all of which had been rejected by every agent in the country. It was only when he'd written the fifth that he had won a publishing deal and it was his seventh book that had been the big one, that one had almost won the Pulitzer. It had been a long hard road, hours and hours of work followed by brutal rejection, but Grose had never given up, never stopped trying. But the students on his course had no sense that writing was craft that had to be honed. All they cared about was getting published and making millions. They wanted to be the next Patterson or Grisham or King or Rowling, they wanted their names on the bestseller lists and their faces on the cover of US magazine and they wanted it right now. The last thing they wanted was to be told that their work was lacking, that they needed to master the basics of storytelling before they could even think about a publishing deal. And because they were themselves too sensitive to criticism they were reluctant to criticize others, so everyone just sat around nodding and smiling and saying how wonderful they all were.

The door to the lecture hall opened and Adrian Slater strode in, his long black coat flapping behind him. He was wearing his impenetrable shades and holding his backpack in his right hand and his motorcycle helmet in his left. "Sorry I'm late, the traffic was a nightmare," he said as headed to the back of the class.

"What do you think you're doing?" asked Grose.

Slater stopped and turned to look at him. "I'm taking my place in class," he said. "I'm sorry to have disturbed your flow."

"Flow? This isn't about flow. You're off this course."

Slater tilted his head to the side. "I don't think so," he said.

"I can assure you that after your performance yesterday I won't be teaching you again."

Slater tilted his chin up. "I don't think you're in a position to make that call," he said. "With respect."

"With respect?" repeated Grose, getting to his feet. "You've shown me not one iota of respect, nor have you shown any respect to the members of this class." He pointed at the door. "I want you to leave, now."

Slater stared at Grose for several seconds and then turned his back on him and walked up to his seat. He sat down, placed his motorcycle helmet and backpack on the floor and folded his arms.

"Mr Slater, I am ordering you to leave the premises. You are off this course."

Slater said nothing.

Grose felt his heart pounding in his chest. Part of him wanted to march up to Slater, grab him by the scruff of the neck and throw him out of the lecture hall, but he knew that in any physical confrontation he'd come off worst. Slater was younger and fitter, and if he refused to go there was nothing that Grose could do about it. "You are in big trouble, Slater," Grose shouted, but even as the words had left his mouth he knew how weak he sounded. He grabbed his briefcase and stormed out, cursing under his breath.

CHAPTER 18

Jenny walked out of the college building with two of her friends but stopped when she saw Slater sitting on a bench on the far side of the road. She had arranged to go shopping with the two girls but changed her mind when she saw that Slater was reading a manuscript. She knew immediately that it was her work in progress that he was reading and she wanted to know what he thought. "I'll catch you later," she said.

"You're not going to talk to him, are you?" asked Rhonda, a tall black girl with dreadlocks that hung half-way down her back. She was from the Bronx and was working on a gritty detective novel with a black lesbian protagonist that Jenny felt was too clichéd to be publishable. Not that she'd ever said that to Rhonda, of course. Most writers pretended to appreciate constructive criticism but deep down all they wanted was to be told how wonderful their work was.

"He's psycho, you know that," said the other girl. Her name was Sally-Anne and she was from a small town in Florida. She was writing about a small girl who was abused by her father and Jenny was fairly sure it was based on Sally-Anne's own experiences. She was stick-thin and had dark patches under her eyes as if she didn't sleep well and while she was often smiling the smile always looked slightly off.

"He's not psycho," said Jenny dismissively.

"He is so psycho," said Rhonda. "He's talking about killing someone on the course, you heard him."

"Doesn't matter anymore anyway," said Sally-Anne. "You heard Grose. He's kicked him off the course. Good riddance, I say. Whether or not he's serious, he shouldn't be screwing with us the way he is. It's not funny."

"He is fit though," said Jenny. "He's got that Robert Pattinson Edward thing going. Mean and moody and soft white skin."

Rhonda faked a shudder. "You are one sick bunny," she said. She nodded at Sally-Anne. "Come on, I hear the Gap calling my name." She reached out and touched Jenny gently on the arm. "Promise me one thing, baby?"

"What?" said Jenny.

"If he does kill you, can I have your laptop? I am so sick of mine freezing on me." She laughed and hurried over the road. He didn't notice her until she sat down on the bench next to him. "Hey," she said.

Slater grinned at her. "How are you doing?"

"I'm fine, but you're still winning friends and influencing people."

"He's an idiot. He can't throw me off the course."

"You just need to handle him the right way."

"Yeah? You know he set the cops on me?" He took out a cigarette and lit it.

"Are you serious?"

Slater nodded and blew smoke. "Two of New York's finest tried to give me the third degree last night."

"What happened?"

"They tried to get heavy with me and they failed miserably," he said. "I sent them packing."

"And you think Dudley sent them?"

"I'm sure of it."

"Why would he do that?"

"I'm guessing he tried to get me thrown off the course and when that didn't work he thought the cops would scare me off." He blew smoke up at the sky. "He thought wrong."

"You shouldn't give Dudley such a hard time. He's a good teacher. Really, he is."

"Maybe. But he's not a writer. Not any more. He's not written anything worth reading since The Snow Birds. His sales have dwindled to pretty much nothing. Some of his books aren't even in print any more. That's why he teaches. Because he can't write. And that doctorate took him six years to get. He's no more a doctor of philosophy than he is a writer."

Jenny looked down at the sidewalk. "He's jealous of you," she said quietly.

"He said that?"

"No. But I know that's why he doesn't like you. You've got something he hasn't." She looked up at him. "Talent."

Slater studied her with amused eyes. Then he slowly grinned. "Do you want to go sailing?"

"Sailing?"

"How can we go sailing? This is New York."

"Which is surrounded by water."

"But where do we get a boat from?"

"I live on a boat."

"You do not."

Slater laughed, took a final drag on his cigarette, and flicked it away in a shower of sparks. "I live on a yacht. For real. Now do you want to come sailing or not?"

CHAPTER 19

Slater drove through the gates to the marina and parked close to a low flat-roofed building with a store at one end and a repair shop at the other. A mechanic in oil-stained overalls waved at Slater as he took off his helmet and Slater waved back. Jenny took off the white motorcycle helmet that Slater had given her and shook her hair. "That was interesting," she said.

"Have you been on a bike before?" asked Slater.

"First time," she said.

Slater grinned mischievously. "That would be why you were hugging me so hard."

"Only when you went fast," she said.

There was a black carrier box on the back and Slater opened it. He took out Jenny's laptop bag and gave it to her, then took the helmet from her and put it in the box and locked it.

"Do you always carry a spare?" she asked.

"Not always."

"But today you happened to have one?"

Slater laughed. "Busted," he said "I was planning on asking you to visit."

"Do people always follow your plans?"

"If I'm lucky," he said. He nodded towards the water. "Come on, I'll show you my pride and joy."

He took her to a wire fence and pulled open a gate and stepped aside to allow her through first. There were more than a hundred boats, most of them motor launches, moored to wooden pontoons, bobbing gently in the grey water.

"I never knew there were marinas in New York," she said as they walked down a narrow pier.

"There's a few," said Slater. "But they cost an arm and a leg."

"And you live on board?"

"Sure." He stopped alongside a single-masted yacht and waved his hand at it. "Home sweet home," he said. Across the stern was the yacht's name. WRITE OF WAY. "Why did you call it that?" asked Jenny.

"Boats are feminine," said Slater. "Never call her 'it'. She's a she."

"Well pardon my lack of knowledge," laughed Jenny. "So why is she called Write Of Way?"

Slater shrugged. "Just a joke, I guess. Plus she's under sail which means powered boats have to give way to her. In theory, anyway."

"What do you mean?"

"Well, the rules of the sea say that a powered boat has to give way to a boat that's under sail. But if a yacht as small as this comes up against a huge freighter or a tanker in the middle of the ocean, the yacht is the one that needs to watch out." He slapped his hands together. "They'd slam right through it and not even notice it."

"Have you been out in the ocean?"

"Sure. Sailed her all the way down to the Panama canal last year and up through the Bahamas and up to New York."

"On your own?"

"Sure."

"That's so cool. I wish I could do something like that."

"You can. You can do anything, Jenny, so long as you set your mind to it." He held out his hand so that he could help her climb onto the deck. Once she was safely on board he joined her and unlocked the padlock that secured the hatch.

"How long have you had her?" asked Jenny.

Slater pulled open the hatch. "A few years," he said. "The great thing is that if you get bored with a place, you just up anchor and go."

"Could you sail across the ocean in her?"

"Sure," said Slater. "You'd want to be careful weather-wise but you could sail around the world if you wanted."

"Are you going to do that one day?"

"Maybe," said Slater. "Would you come?"

Jenny laughed. "I don't think so," she said.

Slater waved at the hatch. "Do you want to have a look below decks?" he asked. "I'll give you the tour. Then we'll take her out."

An hour later they were standing by the wheel, carving through the gently heaving waves of the Hudson River. The nearest vessel was a good quarter of a mile away, a twin-masted yacht heading towards the sea. "Can you take the wheel?" he asked.

"What? Sail her you mean?"

"You'll be fine," said Slater. "The wind's only a couple of knots, we're hardly moving." He put his hands on her hips and guided her to the best position to stand, and showed her the compass. "Keep us on that heading, but don't worry if we move off course. We're sailing so everyone has to give way to you. That's the rule of the sea." He pointed at the GPS monitor. "That's your position there. With this, you can never get lost."

"I thought sailors navigated by the stars and that sextant thing."

"Those days are long gone," said Slater. "I mean, I can use the stars and I do know how to use a sextant but there's no point. You switch on that thing and it tells you where you are to within a few feet."

He patted her on the shoulder and went downstairs into the cabin. He came back up a few minutes later with a bottle of champagne and two glasses. "You're joking," she said.

"What?"

"You can't drink and sail, surely?"

"It's not like driving a car," he said, placing the glasses on the bench seat. "There are no cops with breathalyzers out here." He popped the cork and poured champagne into the glasses. She picked up one of the glasses. He took the other one and clinked it against hers. "To having fun," he said. "To having fun and writing great books."

"And to drinking champagne under sail," she said. She touched her glass against his. "And to good friends."

"Amen to that," he said. They both drank and Slater refilled their glasses.

"I can't believe we're doing this," she said.

"You can do anything you want, Jenny. You just have to put your mind to it."

She waved her glass around. "I mean, this, sailing around Manhattan. Drinking champagne. It's so, I don't know, decadent."

"Decadent?" He waved at the skyscrapers to their right. "That's decadent. Apartments costing tens of millions of dollars, some of the richest people on Earth many of whom haven't worked a day in their lives, churning through the world's resources like there's no tomorrow, while others work all the hours that God sends for minimum wage. This isn't decadent. This is just you and me sharing a bottle of wine on a boat that happens to be my home. This is real."

"It feels real," said Jenny. She sipped her champagne. A seagull swooped over, circled the mast, and then flew off.

"I'm glad you came," said Slater.

"I'm glad I came, too." The wind blew her hair across her face and she shook her head to clear it from her eyes. "So is this going to be in the book?"

Slater studied her with amused eyes. "Do you want it to be?"

She held his look for several seconds and then shook her head. "No."

"Okay then." He looked up at the sail. "The wind's changing, turn to port, just a bit." She turned the wheel and Slater nodded approvingly. "You've really got the hang of it."

Jenny took a deep breath. "Actually I'm feeling a bit queasy." She rubbed her stomach and took another deep breath.

"Keep your eyes on the horizon. It'll help."

Jenny tried that for a few minutes, but then she didn't feel any better. "I'm sorry," she said. "Maybe we should go back."

"Why don't you go below and lie down while I take her in?"

"You don't mind?"

"Don't be silly, you go down below and chill."

Jenny nodded. "Thanks." He helped her through the hatch and she went unsteadily down the stairs. Slater turned the wheel and pointed the yacht towards the marina.

CHAPTER 20

Slater tied up the yacht and then climbed back on to the deck and went down through the hatch. Jenny was lying across the bed. Asleep. He sat down on the bed next to her and brushed her hair from her face. "Hey, sleepyhead, wake up."

She stirred in her sleep but he had to shake her gently to wake her up. "What?" she murmured.

"Time to wake up," he said.

She sat up and ran her hands through her hair. "I still feel a bit sick," she said.

"Do you want some water?"

She shook her head. "Bathroom," she said.

He held her up and guided her to the head. She splashed water on her face while Slater fetched a bottle of water from the fridge. She took several gulps. "Better?" he asked.

She nodded. "I guess I still haven't got my sea legs," she said. She picked up a hairbrush and brushed her hair. She stopped and looked at the bracelet on her wrist. "Oh no, I've lost my charm."

"I wouldn't say that," he said. "At least you didn't throw up."

She held up her left arm. "No, one of my charms has dropped off. A cat."

"I'll check the bed," said Slater. Jenny splashed more water on her face, toweled herself dry, and then went into the main cabin. Slater came out of the sleeping area. "No sign of it," he said. "I hope it didn't come off while you were on the bike. When did you see it last?"

"I put it on first thing this morning and I'm sure it was there then."

"I'll keep looking for it," said Slater. "Come on, I'll drive you home."

"You won't," she said. "You've been drinking. You might be okay handling a yacht with alcohol but you're not driving me through Manhattan on a motorbike."

"Quite right," he said. "I'll call you a cab."

He picked up his cell phone, ordered a cab and walked her to the marina entrance. The office, shop and workshop had closed for the night and he waited with her until a yellow cab arrived.

"I've got something for you," he said, and took a thumbdrive from his pocket. It was in the shape of a hotdog, complete with mustard and ketchup.

"What is it with you and fast food thumbdrives," she said.

"It's The Bestseller," he said. "I want you to read it."

"Am I in it?"

"You're mentioned in passing. Most of the students on the course are."

"And what about today? Will that go in the book?"

"Are you worried about Grose?"

Jenny's face fell. "That's a horrible thing to say."

"But that is the reason, isn't it? You don't want him to know you were on the boat with me."

"I just want what we did today to be personal, between the two of us," she said. "I don't want you reading it out to the whole class."

"I won't," said Slater. "I promise." He opened the rear door of the taxi and she climbed in. "See you in class tomorrow," he said, and closed the door.

He waved with his left hand as the taxi pulled away from the marina. As the cab turned onto the main road he held out his left hand and slowly opened it. Sitting on the palm was a small gold charm. A cat.

CHAPTER 21

Jenny paid the driver, climbed out of the cab and put her hand in her bag for her keys. "Jenny? Where the hell have you been?"

She looked around. Grose was standing at the bottom of the stairs that led up to the front door of her building. "Dudley. What are you doing here?"

"I wanted to surprise you," he said.

"How long have you been here?"

"Half an hour," he said. "Where were you?"

"I was having drinks with some of the girls," she said. "Over on the east side," she added, knowing that he'd be wondering why she'd come back in a cab.

"You didn't answer your cell."

"Battery's dead," she said. "You know me, Dudley, I'm always forgetting to charge it." That was a lie, she'd switched the phone off when she'd gone on board Slater's yacht and forgotten to switch it back on.

"Well, you're here now," he said. He looked at his watch. "But I can't stay long."

She took out her keys and let them into the building and they walked up the stairs together. "Did you have a good time?" he asked.

"It was okay," she said. "I left early, I wasn't feeling so good."

They arrived at her floor and she opened the door to her flat. She put her laptop bag on her desk and then went to get a bottle of wine from the fridge. Grose flopped down onto the sofa and put his feet up on the coffee table. He sighed.

"What's wrong?" asked Jenny, picking up two glasses and pouring wine into them.

"That bastard Slater got a lawyer to call the Head of Faculty."

Jenny stopped in her tracks. "He did what?"

"He got a lawyer to call Kellaway. Threatened the university with a lawsuit if I didn't allow him to attend classes. Kellaway called me into her office and said that Slater has to be allowed to continue. Bitch didn't give me a choice. No argument, no discussion." He sat forward and put his head in his hands. "Bitch, bitch, bitch."

"Oh Dudley, I'm sorry," she said, and sat down next to him.

"I hate this job," said Grose. "I'm not cut out to be a teacher."

She gave him one of the wine glasses. "What about that agent? Has he called?"

"Not yet," said Grose, He sipped his wine.

"You really should think about doing an eBook," she said.

"Oh my God, you and your Kindle," sighed Grose.

"It's not just the Kindle. There are loads of eReaders out there. Sony's got one and so do Barnes & Noble and you can read books on laptops and phones."

"Honey, holding a book and turning the pages is part of the reading experience. It's tactile."

"I'm not saying you should stop writing books, but why don't you think of doing something just as an eBook. No agents, no publishers, you do it yourself. Please say you'll think about it."

He nodded. "Okay."

"Now you're humoring me."

"No. I'll think about it."

"People are selling millions, Dudley. Literally millions."

"Is that what you think writing is all about, Jenny? The money? Am I losing you to the dark side?"

She giggled and put a hand up to cover her mouth.

Grose looked at his watch. "I'm going to have to go."

"Please stay," she said. "I'll cook."

Grose drained his glass and put it on the coffee table. "I can't honey. Maybe on Friday." He stood up. "I'll hopefully be in a better mood by then." He sighed. "I did tell Kellaway that Slater has to start work on a new book and she said she'd talk to him. So hopefully we'll have heard the last of The Bestseller."

CHAPTER 22

Dan Robinson was a big man. He was at least six feet six inches tall with a squarish head and hands the size of shovels. He was reading from his laptop, bent over it and squinting as he read his story out loud. He'd been a construction worker for almost twenty years but had injured his back in an accident and was hoping to earn a living from his writing. It was, Grose knew, the worst possible reason to write. Very few writers made enough from their work to support themselves. The average writer earned a third less than the average worker and the majority of writers earned less than ten thousand dollars a year. Anyone who set out to write to make money was almost certainly doomed to failure. Writers had to write because they wanted to write, was how Grose looked at it. If money and fame came, all well and good. But writing fiction because you wanted to make a fortune was as futile as taking guitar lessons because you wanted to be a rock star.

Yes, there were exceptions, there were writers who sat down to write their way out of poverty. But for every successful writer there were thousands more who struggled along effectively working for less than minimum wage. Grose was pretty sure that was what lay ahead of Robinson, but he forced himself to smile encouragingly as the man read out his work in progress.

Robinson had a soft, gentle voice that was at odds with his appearance. "Her heart pounded and she melted into his arms." He read. "She would give herself to this man, she decided. She would bear his children, she would take care of him, she would die with him. He looked down at her, and kissed her softly on her forehead. She closed her eyes and sighed and she felt his soft lips kiss her again. "I love you," he whispered. "And I always will." She moaned softly and stroked the back of his neck, then, as if it was the most natural thing in the world, she pressed her lips against his and kissed him, finally realizing that he was the man for her, and that he always had been."

Robinson sat back and exhaled, then looked around. Several of the women in the class began to clap and Robinson's cheeks flushed.

"Dan, that was excellent. Really good. It's coming along." That's what Grose said but that wasn't what he thought. It was melodramatic claptrap, the sort of romantic nonsense that his wife enjoyed reading, the literary equivalent of candy floss. "Does anyone else have any thoughts?"

The class spent the next ten minutes offering Robinson advice none of which was remotely critical. Robinson studiously took notes of their comments and thanked everyone for their advice. It was a pointless exercise, Grose knew. Writing, real writing, had to come from the heart, from the soul. Great books weren't written by committee.

Adrian Slater was sitting at the back of the class. He hadn't said a word for three days, just sat there with his impenetrable RayBans making notes. Or drawing cartoons. Grose didn't know which and didn't care. He hadn't been able to force Slater off the course but the Head of Faculty couldn't force Grose to interact with the man. And she couldn't force him to pass Slater. It gave Grose some small satisfaction to know that it didn't matter how many hours Slater spent in class, he was still going to fail.

Grose looked at his watch. There was still twenty minutes to go. He put on his spectacles and looked around the class. "Well, who else is ready to share their work with us?" Perhaps something this time without vampires or love-struck maidens or talking dogs."

Stan Naghdi raised his hand but Grose pointedly ignored him. He really didn't want to listen to Naghdi's attempt at science fiction again. He looked towards the back of his class and his stomach lurched when he saw Slater get to his feet, holding a sheath of papers. "I have something I'd like to share with the class, Doctor Grose," he said.

Grose's jaw tightened. The last thing he wanted was for Slater to read out his work, even Naghdi's Star Trek rip-off would be preferable. But if he refused to allow Slater to participate there was a good chance that he, or his lawyer, would complain to the Head of Faculty. Grose slowly removed his glasses. "Go ahead, Mr Slater," he said, wearily.

The class fell silent and the students at the front, including Jenny, twisted around to get a better look at Slater. He cleared his throat, and began to read.

"I've worked out where to bury the victim's body parts. Good places, places where they'll never be found by accident. And I've put together the clues, just like a treasure hunt. Now all I need is the victim."

Grose sighed and rubbed the bridge of his nose. He'd made his mind up just to let Slater get on with it. He was going to be failing the course anyway.

"The key now is to find the victim, and follow her. So lately I've been practicing because it's not easy to follow people. Not one on one. The professionals, the FBI and the cops and the DEA and the CIA, they use teams. Six or more. That's how many you need to follow someone. Ideally you need people on foot and a couple of cars. The best way by far is to have a GPS on the target or the target's car, but that's not something I'm going to be able to do."

Grose sighed and shook his head.

"I need to hone my skills. I need to learn how to follow someone without them knowing. It's a skill, the skill of a predator and it's a skill I'm starting to learn. That's one of the reasons I've chosen New York. It's the most populous city in the world. It's a funny word, populous. It means there are a lot of people. About twenty million. But it's a city of individuals. Of strangers. Most of them are so wrapped up in their own little lives that they don't pay attention to what's going on around them. As they walk around they talk on their cell phones, listen to their MP-3 players, or are just lost in their own thoughts. They tend not to look at strangers because strangers might be a threat and threats are best ignored. Eye contact can lead to confrontation and in New York confrontation can lead to death. So everyone hurries around, protected by their own bubble of indifference."

Grose looked at his watch and sighed again. "Is there much more of this, Mr Slater?"

Slater ignored him and continued to read. "I've already found a girl who I think will be perfect. So I followed her to her apartment in Chelsea, not far from the Garment District. I did it on foot, twice, following her at a distance. I followed her right to the door and she never knew. I spent time outside the building, getting to know the area. And that's when I saw her lover, paying her a visit. Her lover's an older man, old enough to be her father."

Grose stiffened and Jenny turned around to look at him, her mouth open in horror.

"So then I got to thinking, maybe I'd follow the lover. I wanted to see how good my tailing skills were. Could I follow her lover home? What could I discover about her lover's home life. It was a challenge and if there's one thing that a predator relishes, it's a challenge. So I waited outside and followed him when he left. I kept well back and followed him to Penn Station and saw which train he boarded. The second evening I was already at the station with a ticket and I got on the train with him. He was reading a book and didn't look up once but even if he had he wouldn't have seen me because I was in the next car. I saw which station he got off at but I stayed on the train and got off at the next station and headed back to Manhattan. On the third day I was waiting at the station on my motorbike. Black leathers and a full face helmet. But again he wasn't looking around so he didn't give me a second glance."

Slater stopped and looked at Grose as if daring him to comment. Grose knew that there was nothing he could say that would stop what was about to happen. Slater sneered and continued to read.

"He waited outside the station for almost ten minutes. He wasn't happy at being kept waiting, I could see that. Paced up and down. Kept looking at his watch. Eventually a white SUV pulled up. One of those Korean models. There was a woman driving. His wife, I guess. He got in and kissed her and off they went. I followed them. Not difficult on a bike, the trick was to stay far enough away that she wouldn't see me. But then most people rarely use their mirrors on quiet roads. They listen to their music or talk on the phone or get lost in their thoughts. Cars are the biggest bubbles going.

"They drove for about twenty minutes and stopped in front of a pretty colonial house, pale green with a steep pitched roof, two chimneys and a wide porch with a swing seat on it. They parked outside and I watched as they went in. I sat and waited. I guess they had dinner or drinks or something because the lights stayed on downstairs until just before eleven thirty when they went off and a light went on in one of the bedroom windows."

Grose stood up. "I think that's probably enough, Mr Slater, don't you?"

"I was just getting into my stride," said Slater. He held up the sheets of paper. "I've quite a bit to go." He smiled. "I'm sure the Head of Faculty would want me to continue, don't you?"

Grose stared stonily at Slater as he sat down. He waved for Slater to continue.

"I waited until the bedroom light had been off for half an hour and then I took a walk around the house. There's very little crime in upstate New York and people don't always lock their doors. This guy didn't anyway. The kitchen door wasn't locked or bolted and I went inside. There's nothing like the feeling of sneaking into someone else's home, especially when they're upstairs asleep. You get to move through their territory, touch their most treasured possessions, to root through their secrets. The house was full of books. Books everywhere. Mainly cheap romances, the sort with bare-chested men holding big-bosomed women with doe-like eyes. I guess that's what the wife reads. I'm guessing she doesn't have much romance in her life so she looks for it in fiction."

Grose got to his feet again. This time he walked purposefully towards Slater. "You think this is funny, Slater?" he shouted. "You think you get away with threatening me like this?"

Slater grinned but didn't say anything.

"Give me that," shouted Grose, holding out his hand. "Give that crap to me now."

Slater shook his head.

"I insist that you give it to me now," shouted Grose.

"It's my work in progress," said Slater quietly. "I'm happy to read it to the class but I'm not prepared to give it to you." He rolled up the papers and put them into his backpack.

Grose tried to grab the backpack but Slater moved it away from him. Grose roared in frustration. Slater was younger and fitter and there was nothing he could do to exert his authority. He felt tears prick his eyes and he clenched his fists tightly. He stood staring at Slater, breathing heavily. Then he turned and walked down to his table, picked up his briefcase and walked out, blinking away the tears.

CHAPTER 23

Jenny found Grose in the cafeteria, nursing a cup of coffee. "Are you okay, Dudley?" she asked. He ignored her and continued to stare at the table. She sat down opposite him. "He shouldn't have said that," she said. "What he did was horrible."

"Now do you believe me?" he said, still refusing to look at her. "He's a psychopath. He doesn't care who he hurts."

"Do you think he really followed you home?"

He lifted his head and stared at her. "What do you think?" he said coldly.

"The way he described your wife. That's not how you talk about her. And he said you kissed her on the cheek. You said you never kissed her."

"It was a peck. A peck on the cheek. Hardly a kiss."

"So he was there? He went to your house?"

Grose shook his head contemptuously. "You're finally starting to understand, aren't you?"

"I can't believe he was outside my apartment block. And he saw you. Why would he do that?"

"He's a psychopath. There's no point in asking why." Grose reached over and held her hands. "I don't want you going near him, Jenny. Do you hear? Keep away from him."

Two girls giggled as they walked by the table and Grose pulled his hands away.

Jenny reached into her laptop bag and took out the hotdog thumbdrive that Slater had given her. "Dudley, you need to read this."

"What is it?"

"Slater's work in progress. The Bestseller."

Grose took it from her, his forehead creased into deep frowns. "How long have you had this?"

"Not long," she said.

"Have you read it?"

"I haven't had time," she said. "But I think you should." That was a lie. She'd read it on her laptop the first chance she'd got because she'd wanted to see what Slater had said about her. Other than a couple of mentions of the work she'd read in class, there was nothing. Most of the manuscript was Slater's thoughts on life and death and killing. And after she'd read it she'd come to the conclusion that Grose was right – Slater was a psychopath. Good-looking and charming, but clearly disturbed and dangerous.

Grose nodded. He held the thumbdrive tightly as if he feared she'd change her mind and take it back.

"What are you going to do, Dudley?"

"I've got to talk to the Dean," he said. "And the police. If someone doesn't do something Slater's going to commit murder, I'm sure of it." He pushed back his chair and stood up. "I'm serious about this, Jenny, you stay away from him." He hurried out of the cafeteria, his fist clenched around the thumbdrive.

CHAPTER 24

The faculty secretary was adding numbers to a spreadsheet when Grose walked in. She looked up and smiled. Her name was Marion and she was a fan and at least once a month would remind him that Snow Birds was her all time favorite novel. "Marion, can you do me a big favor?" he asked.

"Of course, Dudley," she said.

Grose held out the hotdog thumbdrive. "There's a file on this. The Bestseller. Do you think you could print it out for me."

"You really do hate computers, don't you?" she laughed. She took the thumbdrive from him and plugged it into the side of her computer. Her fingers played over the keyboard and a few seconds later the printer behind her kicked into life. Marion peered at the screen. "Forty-two pages," she said.

"Thanks, Marion," he said. As he looked over at the printer he noticed a grey plastic oblong sticking out of her bag.

She saw him looking at it and took it out. "It's a Kindle," she said. "My new toy. My husband bought it for my birthday and I use it all the time. I don't think I've bought a real book since I got it." She held it out to him and he took it.

"But don't you miss holding a real book?" he said.

"Oh I do, but you soon get used to it." She took it from him and held it to her bosom. Her face went suddenly serious. "Oh, but did you know that your books aren't available on Kindle ? Why is that?"

"I don't know," said Grose.

"You really should talk to your publisher. I'd love a copy of Snow Birds on mine."

"I'll do that. But please tell me that you'll keep buying real books."

"Oh, I'm sure I will," she said. "It's not great for cookbooks because you wouldn't want to get it dirty in the kitchen, and it doesn't do pictures very well. But you know I love romance novels and it's perfect for that. Do you know how many books I have on my baby?"

"I've no idea," said Grose.

"Have a guess. Go on, have a guess."

Grose was getting tired of the conversation but she was doing him a favor so he forced a smile. "Fifty?"

"More," she said.

"A hundred?"

"A hundred and twelve," she said. "Can you believe that ? And most of them are free. All the classics are free."

"Because they're out of copyright," said Grose.

"I just downloaded the complete works of Sherlock Holmes. Totally free."

"You mean the complete works of Sir Arthur Conan Doyle," said Grose. "Sherlock Holmes was the character."

Marion seemed oblivious to the correction as she continued to extol the merits of eBooks, caressing her Kindle as she spoke. Grose nodded politely until the printer stopped spewing out sheets. Marion gathered them together and handed them to him. He thanked her and hurried out of the office. He found an empty lecture room and sat down and started reading.

CHAPTER 25

Grose burst into the Dean's office, waving the manuscript. "Now you've got to believe me," he said. The Dean's secretary followed him, apologizing profusely.

"It's all right, Isabel, I can see Dr Grose now," she said. The secretary closed the door, still apologizing.

"Dudley, you really can't come charging into my office like this," said the Dean.

Grose slapped Slater's manuscript onto the Dean's desk. "It's all in here," he said. "How he's going to choose a victim, kill her and dismember the body. He describes buying a set of knives and a book on anatomy. He talks about cutting the body into pieces and burying them all around the State."

"Dudley, sit down. And calm down. You look like you're about to have a stroke." She waved at one of the chairs facing her desk.

Grose sat down and jabbed a finger at the manuscript. "That is a blueprint for murder," he said.

"But it's a work of fiction, isn't it? You're teaching a creative writing course. Mr Slater is being creative. He hasn't actually killed anyone, has he?"

"Because he hasn't finished the book yet. Look, he sits at the back of the class dressed in black wearing sunglasses. He's clearly got mental health issues."

"Now you want to throw him off the course because of his fashion choices? Dudley half our students wear black."

"But half the students aren't writing a do-it-yourself guide to murder."

The Dean picked up the manuscript and flicked through it. "If he really was planning a murder based on his book, he'd hardly give it to you to read, would he?"

"Dean Martin, Slater just announced to the class that he'd followed me back to my home. That he's spied on me and my wife."

"He mentioned you by name?"

"No. He didn't have to. It was obviously me."

"Well even if it was, Dudley, there are plenty of examples of novelists using real people in their books. Fictionalized histories. And what about faction where factual events are fictionalized. That's a whole new genre."

"I'm running a creative writing course," snapped Grose.

"Exactly," said the Dean. "And that's what he's doing. He's being creative." Grose opened his mouth to speak but the Dean raised a ring-encrusted hand to silence him. "Dudley, before you dig yourself any deeper, let me tell you that two days ago Mr Slater was in to see me." She flashed him a tight smile. "And unlike you he had the good manners to make an appointment. He wanted to talk about the problems he'd been having on the course, and that you appeared to be running some sort of vendetta against him."

"A vendetta?"

"He felt that your relationship had got off on the wrong foot and that you were being overly-critical of his work."

"That's bullshit," said Grose.

"There's no need for profanity, Dudley. And Mr Slater might well feel that you were being too harsh in your criticism. He discussed the plot of his novel with me and it's clearly a work of fiction. It's a serial killer book but written in the first person."

"You've fallen for his...." Grose trailed off. He'd been about to say "bullshit" again.

"Think American Psycho, Dudley. And think how the university would benefit if one of our students would turn out to be the new Bret Easton Ellis."

"And think what it would mean if one of our students turned out to be the new Ted Bundy," said Grose. He took a deep breath. "Did you read his manuscript?"

"No, I didn't."

"Well you should. You should read it. Then you'd realize what a psycho he is."

The Dean's eyes narrowed. "How did you get the manuscript, Dudley? I did ask him if I could read it and he said he didn't want to show it to anyone until it was finished."

"I'd rather not say."

"Are you telling me that he doesn't know you have it?"

"The important thing is what he says in the book. He's talking about killing a student."

"Dudley, I'm going to ask you one more time. How did you get the manuscript?"

Grose gritted his teeth as he realized that there was no way that he could tell the Dean that Jenny had given it to him. That would open up a whole can of worms. He reached out and took it from her. "Fine," he said. "Just forget I mentioned it. But mark my words, Adrian Slater is a dangerous piece of work. And if this pans out the way I think it will, you and this university could be facing a massive legal action."

The Dean frowned and Grose realized that he'd finally got her attention. "What do you mean?"

Grose shoved the manuscript into his jacket pocket. "I mean that if Slater does carry out his threat, the family of any victim would be able to sue the university. And you."

"It's a novel, Dudley. Mr Slater has assured me that it's a work of fiction."

"And you believe him?"

"You are teaching a creative writing course, remember?"

"And I want him off it," said Grose.

"It's not as simple as that," said the Dean. "Mr Slater has already made it clear that if we refuse to allow him to continue on the course, he will sue us. We can't afford that. And we can't afford the negative publicity it would generate."

"So you're backing him against me? Is that it?"

"It's not a question of taking sides. It's about doing what's best for the university. And the simple fact is that we can't exclude him from the course because we don't like what he's writing. There are First Amendment issues at stake and that's not a fight that I'm prepared to get into."

Grose rubbed the back of his neck and his hand came away wet. He hadn't realized how much he'd been sweating. He stood up. "There's nothing else to say then, is there?"

"Not really, no."

"Be it on your head," said Grose.

"Dudley, you need to take a deep breath and put this into perspective," said the Dean.

Grose shook his head in disgust and walked out of her office.

CHAPTER 26

Mitchell and Lumley watched Slater drive up on his high-powered motorcycle and they walked over to him as he climbed off and removed his motorcycle helmet. "You just don't get it, do you?" said Mitchell. They were in a car park a short walk from the Faculty building.

Slater smiled amiably. "Good morning officers," he said. "What brings you out so early? Donut run?"

"Doctor Grose called us. Seems you broke into his house," said Mitchell.

Slater laughed. "Dr Grose really needs to start separating fact from fiction." He looked at his watch. "Now if you don't mind, I've got a lecture to go to."

"We do mind," said Mitchell. "In fact we'd like to talk to you, down at the station."

"About what?" asked Slater.

"About the meaning of life, what do you think we want to talk to you about?" said Lumley. She had her hair tied back in a ponytail and was holding her coat open so that anyone who walked by could see the detective's badge hanging around her neck.

"There'll be coffee, right?" said Slater. "And donuts."

"Just get in the car, Slater," said Lumley, gesturing at a nondescript car behind them.

"You're not arresting me, are you?"

"No," said Mitchell. "We just need to talk."

"I guess I can spare the time," said Slater. "Plus it's all good research."

"Research for what?" asked Lumley.

"My book," said Slater. "I'm about to write an interrogation scene so this'll help me get my facts right. You guys still use telephone books right?"

"What?" said Lumley.

"Telephone books? You hit suspects with them to beat the truth out of them. Telephone books don't leave marks, right?"

"You've a very funny man," growled Mitchell. "Come on."

"I call shotgun," said Slater, heading towards their car.

CHAPTER 27

Mitchell slowly sipped his coffee, his eyes fixed on Slater's face. "Please remove your sunglasses, Mr Slater," he said.

Slater pushed them up so that they were perched on the top of his head. "Don't I get a coffee?" asked Slater.

"No," said Mitchell.

Slater looked across at Lumley. "Assuming you're playing good cop-bad cop, how about a cup of joe, Joe?"

"Eat shit and die, Slater," said Lumley.

"So this is what, bad cop and even worse cop?"

"So now you're breaking into houses, are you?" said Mitchell.

Slater shrugged.

"You broke into Dr Grose's house," said Mitchell.

"Proof?"

"Proof?" repeated Mitchell.

"Proof," said Slater. "The evidence or argument that compels the mind to accept an assertion as true. That's the dictionary definition. Where's your proof?"

"You told a room full of students what you'd done." Lumley pushed a plastic evidence bag across the table towards him. Inside was a manuscript. His manuscript. "This is the book that you're working on."

Slater nodded at the manuscript. "That doesn't say anything about breaking into Doctor Grose's house. And you know it doesn't. Assuming you read it." He grinned. "Assuming that you can read."

You left these in the lecture hall when Doctor Grose threw you out."

Slater folded his arms and slouched in his seat. He sighed and looked up at the ceiling. "This is so old," he said. "How many times do I have to tell you? It's a novel. A work of fiction."

"A novel?" said Mitchell. He tapped the evidence bag. "A novel? Is that what you call it? You talk about stalking a fellow student and killing her. You talk about dismembering the body and hiding the parts all over the State."

Slater smirked. "I've got a vivid imagination."

Mitchell looked at him coldly. "I suppose you got that from your father."

Slater froze and Mitchell felt his heart race. Slater tried to smile, but it was too late, Mitchell knew that he'd touched a nerve.

"This is all a waste of time," said Slater. "I'm writing a novel. You can't keep arresting me every time one of my characters breaks the law. What are you planning to do next? Arrest Jeffrey Deaver? Thomas Harris? Patricia Cornwell? Michael Connolly? Are you going to charge them with murder because they write about serial killers?"

Mitchell stared at Slater for several seconds. "Not embarrassed of your father, are you, Slater? A talent like his, I would have thought you'd have been proud to be his son."

Slater sneered at the sergeant. "So now suddenly you're the great detective?"

"And you're the great writer? Like your father?"

Slater glared at Mitchell and then slowly pulled his RayBans down over his eyes.

"Take them off," said Mitchell.

"Make me," said Slater.

Mitchell started to reach for the glasses but then stopped. He shrugged. "I don't need to see your eyes to know when you're lying, Slater." He sipped his coffee. "Can't be easy, living in his shadow. You wanting to be a writer so badly."

"I am a writer," said Slater quietly.

Mitchell shook his head. "No, your father was a writer. A great writer. Three Pulitzer nominations and he won it once. All of his books are still in print, which is good going considering he's been dead for what, ten years?"

"Nine," said Slater.

"Moved to Los Angeles in the early Eighties," said Mitchell, leaning forward and lowering his voice. "That's where he killed himself, isn't it?"

Slater's lips were pressed together so tightly that they had almost disappeared.

"Manic depressive, wasn't he? Ups and downs. Can't have been an easy man to live with. Is that why you changed your name?"

Still Slater said nothing. He lowered his head so that his chin touched his chest. Mitchell couldn't tell if Slater's eyes were open or closed behind the impenetrable lenses.

"Or did you just think that Slater was a better pen name?"

"It's my real name. It was a legal change."

"Oh, I know that. Passport, driver's license. You are Adrian Slater, no doubt about that. But of course there's no birth certificate and no record of you before you were eighteen. That's when you became Adrian Slater. Before that you were Adrian Henderson." Mitchell grinned. "What, did you think we wouldn't find out? Do you think you could keep your little secret? This isn't a novel, Slater. This is the real world, and in the real world detectives detect."

Mitchell sipped his coffee again. Slater looked at his watch.

"We're not keeping you, are we, Slater?" said Mitchell, putting his coffee back on the table. He sat back in his chair and interlinked his fingers. "Funny that he didn't leave a note," he said. "Him being a writer and all. You'd think he'd want to leave some last words. A message to you, maybe.

Or his wife." Mitchell frowned. "Oh, but she was in hospital wasn't she? When he shot himself in the head."

Slater said nothing.

"So why do you think he did a Hemingway, Adrian? His books were doing great, he was one of the most sought-after American writers. Was that it, do you think? He wanted to go out at the top? Couldn't face the long slow slide back into obscurity?"

"I don't think about it, much," said Slater quietly.

"Oh come on, of course you think about it. You're a teenager and your dad kills himself. You'd have to wonder why. Maybe blame yourself a little? Maybe think that if you'd been a better son he wouldn't have done it. Those sorts of thoughts would only be natural. Understandable."

There was a long silence as the two men stared at each other.

"What happened to your mother, Adrian?" asked Lumley, breaking the silence.

"I'm sure it's in the file."

"I haven't read it." She looked across at Mitchell. "This is the first I've heard of it."

"So this is what? Informed cop and stupid cop? Do these games actually work?"

"This is the first I've heard about your mother," said Lumley. "First I've heard of your father, too. Looks like I'm playing catch-up at the moment."

"Been keeping your cards close to your chest, Ed?" asked Slater. "What's the problem? Don't you trust Joe?"

"Tell us what happened to your mother," said Mitchell. "Or do you want me to? It's just that I'd hate to get any of the details wrong."

Slater glared at Mitchell, then turned his head to look at Lumley. "My mother has mental health issues," he said. "It started when she was pregnant with me and got worse as I was growing up. She was in and out of hospitals.

All private, my father paid whatever needed paying to make sure that she got the best treatment."

"But the treatment didn't help, did it?" said Mitchell. "Nutty as a fruitcake, right?"

Slater ignored Mitchell and continued to look at Lumley. "She started self-harming after my father died. She hasn't left the hospital since it happened."

"It can't have been easy. Your father killing himself and your mother sick like that."

Slater leaned forward, towards her. "Don't bother trying to empathize with me. You're wasting your time. I'm a writer. I spend a lot of time getting into the heads of my characters. So I can see what you're trying to do and I'm just telling you, it won't work."

"There's no need to be so sensitive, Adrian," said Mitchell. He pointed at Slater's head. "I really want to know what's going on in there. There's something not quite right, we both know that. It's probably in the DNA. Your father kills himself and your mother's a Fruit Loop. With the best will in the world you were never going to turn out right, were you?"

Slater sat back and folded his arms. "I'm done talking," he said.

CHAPTER 28

Mitchell and Lumley watched through the window as five floors below Slater crossed the road, his black coat flapping behind him. His trademark RayBans were back on and as he reached the sidewalk he stopped and lit a cigarette.

"He enjoys playing with us, you know that," said Lumley.

"Give him enough rope and he'll hang himself," said Mitchell.

"What do you mean, Ed? You want him to kill, is that what you're saying?"

Mitchell looked across at her, his eyes narrowing. "Where did that come from, Joe?"

Lumley put up a hand. "I'm not arguing with you, I'm just saying we're not doing a great job of warning him off, are we?"

Down below Slater turned and looked up at their window. He grinned and flashed them a mock salute. Mitchell made a gun of his right hand, pointed it at Slater and mimed firing it. Slater did the same with his left hand as he blew smoke, then walked off down the street.

"Bastard," said Mitchell.

"And what was that about his father? Why didn't you tell me Slater wasn't his real name?"

"Only found out just before I went into the interrogation room. Got an email from Los Angeles PD."

"A heads-up would have been nice," said Lumley. "So who was the father?"

"Ben Henderson. Wrote a slew of action movies but before he went Hollywood he won a Pulitzer for a book he wrote. Summer Sons, remember?"

"I'm not a big reader," said Lumley.

"Me neither, but I remember Oprah raving about it. Blew his head off with a shotgun."

"That'll do it," said Lumley.

"What with that and his mother in the nuthouse, it's hardly surprising that Slater's turned out to be such a psycho."

There was a coffeemaker on top of a filing cabinet by the door and Lumley went over to get herself a fresh coffee. "You want one?" she asked Mitchell.

Mitchell shook his head. "Doctor says I've got to cut down." He grimaced. "What the hell, go on. What do doctors know, right?"

Lumley made two mugs of coffee. Black with one sugar for Mitchell, just a splash of milk for her. "Ed, do you really think that Slater is a potential killer?"

"You've spoken to him, what do you think?"

"Until you dropped the bombshell about his parents I was coming around to thinking that he's all talk."

"And now?"

Lumley carried over the coffees and gave Mitchell his mug. "The father's death, it definitely was self-inflicted?"

"I've only just got the email, but I would have thought the LAPD would have been pretty thorough if a high-profile was found dead. Why, are you thinking Slater might have killed his father?"

"The mum blames the dad, resentment simmers over the years, the boy becomes a man and takes his revenge."

"Are you serious, Joe?"

Lumley frowned as she sipped her coffee. "He's either a stone-cold sociopath or he's a smartass who gets a kick out of giving us the runaround. There's no real middle ground here. He's either a killer, potential or otherwise, or he's a writer who's pushing the creative envelope and forcing us to be part of that. My money's on the sociopath."

Mitchell sat down. "I think you mean psychopath, don't you?"

"Same thing, right?" said Lumley. "What is it the experts call it? Anti-Social Personality Disorder? Someone who causes pain to others without feeling any guilt."

"Yeah, but the last time I was on a psych course they were saying that sociopaths are disorganized and psychopaths are organized. So a sociopath will act rashly and make an extreme response to a normal situation, as if their impulse control has been switched off."

Lumley's jaw dropped in surprise. "Are you shitting me?" she said.

Mitchell grinned. "Hey, the woman giving the lecture had a great rack, what can I say? I paid attention and I asked questions. "But she said that psychopaths were more organized and often fantasized about their acts before carrying them out. And that's what Slater's doing, right? He's writing down what he plans to do, which is about as organized as you can get. Anyway he's a psychopath. Doesn't matter what's on the label just so long as we put him away."

"Except he hasn't actually done anything yet, has he?"

"Yeah, well I'm gonna get his file and go through it line by line. Back then they were probably treating him like a distraught family member, it might start to look different if we're thinking of him as a cold, hard killer."

"So we go through his file and bring him back in, is that the plan?"

"Sure, but when we do, keep your distance," warned Mitchell.

"What do you mean?"

"Psychopaths can be charming. Charismatic. Manipulative. That's how they get close to their victims."

Lumley's eyes narrowed. "What are you saying, Ed? I'm a moth to his flame, is that what you think?"

"I'm just saying be careful, that's all."

"I'm not the victim type, Ed," she said. "Never have been, never will be."

CHAPTER 29

Grose's cell phone rang and he took it out of his jacket pocket. He was sitting in the Faculty library, reading through Slater's manuscript again. He had given the original copy to the two detectives but had been back into the Faculty office and asked Marion to print him another copy from the thumbdrive. As he read he sucked on the end of his Mont Blanc fountain pen. He was trying to pin down dates and times so that he could see about proving that Slater had been following him. He looked at the phone's screen. It was a cell phone but he didn't recognise the number. He took the call.

"Dr Grose, this is Detective Lumley, NYPD."

"Yes Detective. What's happening? Is he under arrest?"

"We had Mr Slater in for an interview but that's now come to an end. We're satisfied that we've done all that we can so far."

"He's not in jail?"

"It doesn't work like that, Dr Grose. It's going to take time to build a case."

"What about conspiracy to murder?"

"You need more than one person to have a conspiracy, Dr Grose."

"He's planning a murder. Doesn't that count for something? And he was in my house. What's that, trespass? Can't you charge him with trespass?"

"We don't have any evidence that he was actually inside your house."

"You have his manuscript. His work in progress. He describes me, he describes my wife, our car and our house. What more do you need?"

"We need hard evidence, Dr Grose."

"So come and check for fingerprints at my house."

"He said he was driving his motorcycle. So he'd be wearing gloves."

Grose cursed. "So you're saying that's it? There's nothing you can do?"

"Not at the moment. But we will be watching him. And if he does in any way threaten you again, let us know."

"So you haven't done anything, basically."

"Dr Grose, Adrian Slater hasn't committed an offence. We've spoken to him, we've warned him...."

"Warned him!" shouted Grose. Several students turned to look at him and Grose lowered his voice and cupped his hand over the phone. "He's planning to kill one of my students and you've warned him! Christ, woman, can't you see what he's up to?"

"I understand how upset you are, Dr Grose....."

"I don't want your understanding, Detective. I want you to do something. He's going to kill a girl and dismember her, and he's going to bury the bits in some sort of psychopathic treasure hunt."

"Dr Grose, please…"

Grose ended the call and banged the phone down on the table. Two students at a neighboring table turned to look at him and he glared back. "What?" he shouted. "What the fuck are you looking at?"

CHAPTER 30

Andrew Yates lay with his eyes closed listening to the girl breathing next to him. What was her name? Lisa? Linda? Laura? Something beginning with L. Lindsay? Yes, Lindsay felt right. From Ohio. Or Omaha. She was a paralegal. Fragments of the previous evening began to fall into place. He'd met her at a bar in 53rd Street. He'd been with three of his friends from the office, she'd been with a married girlfriend who had a husband waiting for her so when the friend left Lindsay had tagged along with Andrew and his group. No, not Lindsay. Leena. Definitely Leena. They'd hit another bar and then Andrew's friends had taken the hint and left them to it. He'd bought her a burger and then more drinks and then gone to a club where he'd given her an ecstasy tablet and taken one himself and that was pretty much all he could remember. No, not Leena. Elle. Her name was Elle. Or was that her nickname and Leena was her full name. That felt right. Her name was Leena but everyone called her Elle.

He looked at his watch. Half past eight. It was Saturday so he didn't have to get to work but his wife was due in at noon, back from a two-day sales conference in Seattle. He had to be at the airport to meet her or there'd be hell to pay. He tried to remember what had happened after he'd got back to Elle's room. There had been sex, he remembered that much. And she'd had some coke, which had been nice and a surprise. She'd had a drawer full of sex toys as well, which had been less nice. He could never understand girls who wanted to bring sex toys into the bed when they had full use of the real thing. He just hoped that she hadn't marked him. He hadn't felt any scratches and he hadn't let her get her mouth anywhere near his neck just in case she'd thought that biting was sexy.

Elle moved in her sleep and Yates edged his body away from hers. She didn't look half as attractive in the cold light of day. Her mascara had smudged and her cheeks were peppered with small white spots and for the first time he noticed the brown roots of her dyed hair. She told him that she was twenty-eight but in the cold light of day she looked closer to her mid-thirties, almost as old as his wife.

He rolled out from under the duvet, slowly so as not to wake her, gathered up his shoes and clothes and carried them to the bathroom. He draped his clothes over the side of the bath and looked at his reflection in the mirror above the sink. He ran his hand over the stubble on his chin and decided to shave. If one of the neighbors saw him going into his apartment looking as if he'd been out all night then tongues would start wagging. Especially old Mrs Wilkinson who lived next door. She'd always hated him since he'd complained about her yapping Yorkshire Terrier and she'd relish the opportunity of telling his wife that he'd been out all night. He looked around for shaving foam but there was a lady razor in the shower so he took it and splashed water on his face and then used a bar of soap to work up a lather. He looked at his watch again. He had more than enough time to pop into a convenience store on the way home so that anyone who saw him would just assume he'd popped out for some shopping.

"Andrew, are you okay?"

Yates flinched as he heard Elle's voice. He had hoped to get out without waking her. "I'm fine, baby. Just shaving."

"Do you want coffee? Or green tea?"

"Coffee would be great, baby. Two sugars and milk, please."

Yates gritted his teeth. Now he was going to have to talk to her before making his excuses and getting the hell out of her apartment. He stared at his reflection as he ran the small plastic razor down his cheek but flinched when a smear of red appeared. Blood. He cursed under his breath. He wasn't used to wet shaving, he'd used an electric razor for years. He started to shave under his chin and as he ran the razor along the soapy skin a second blob of blood appeared high up on his cheek.

He took a step back, frowning. As he looked quizzically at his reflection a small drop of blood splattered on the side of the sink. Yates looked at the razor in his hand, then back at the red smear on the sink. That didn't make any sense. He slowly looked up and gasped when he saw the wet scarlet patch in the ceiling above his head.

CHAPTER 31

Ed Mitchell showed his badge to a bored uniform cop standing guard at the entrance to the apartment. The cop nodded and stepped to the side. Lumley was standing in the hallway, scribbling in her notebook. "It's Saturday, Joe," he said. "I don't do Saturdays."

"You'll want this one, Ed," she said, looking up from her notebook. She was wearing a black suit with a long jacket that reached almost to her knees and she'd tied her hair back with a scrunchy.

Mitchell looked over her shoulder into a white-tiled bathroom where two CSU investigators in pale blue paper suits were taking photographs and sketching the area. Even from where he was standing Mitchell could see that the floor was awash with blood.

"They're doing the second walk-through," said Lumley.

"Where's the body?" asked Mitchell.

"That's a very good question, Ed."

"Please tell me that you haven't called me in on a Saturday and there's no body?"

"There's a lot of blood but no corpse."

Mitchell sighed. "Today's the day I get to take my boy out," he said. "Two Saturdays a month."

"Your boys fifteen, Ed," said Lumley, "and you're always bitching about how much he hates you. The apartment's rented by a Jenny Cameron."

Mitchell frowned. The name meant nothing.

"She's on Doctor Grose's creative writing course," said Lumley.

"You're shitting me," said Mitchell.

"Sadly, I'm not," said Lumley, putting away her notebook. Her badge was hanging from a thin steel chain around her neck.

"And the body's gone?"

"Not so much as a fingernail."

Mitchell grimaced. "How much blood is that, do you think?" he asked one of the CSU investigators, a middle-aged man with thinning hair and a potbelly straining at the waist of his paper suit.

"A body's worth, pretty much," said the man.

Mitchell nodded. "So he takes the body away but doesn't clear up the blood. Doesn't care that we know that he killed her." He looked over at Lumley. "Any sign of the knife?"

"There's a knife block in the kitchen but all the knives are accounted for. He did it, didn't he?"

"Who did it?" asked the CSU investigator. "Husband? Boyfriend?"

"A writer," said Mitchell. "He killed her and butchered her and now he's hidden the body parts."

"Are you serious?" asked the man.

"As serious as cancer," said Mitchell. He looked at Lumley again. "Let's go get the bastard."

CHAPTER 32

Slater sat back in his chair. His RayBans were perched on the back of his head. It was just after seven in the evening and Mitchell and Lumley had left him on his own in the interview room for the best part of two hours. It was a standard technique, letting the suspect worry about what was going to happen. But it didn't seem to have fazed Slater in the least and he grinned at them as they took their places on the opposite side of the table.

Mitchell stared at Slater impassively for several seconds before speaking. "When was the last time you saw Jenny Cameron?"

Slater shrugged. "A few days ago. I'm not sure. Last time I was in Grose's class, I guess."

"What about her apartment? When was the last time you were there?"

"Never been to her place."

"You sure about that?" asked Mitchell.

"It's not the sort of thing I'd forget," said Slater. "She's fit, is Jenny Cameron."

"She gets your pulse racing, does she?" asked Lumley.

Slater grinned at her. "Not as much as you do, Joe."

"Detective Lumley to you," she said.

"I thought we'd moved beyond the formal stage," he said.

Mitchell pointed his finger at Slater. "If you were in that apartment, the CSU guys will find out. And then we'll have you."

"CSU? Don't you mean CSI?"

"What?" said Mitchell.

"I thought it was CSI. Like the TV show."

"In New York it's the Crime Scene Unit. CSU. You don't want to believe everything you see on the TV, Slater. Real CSU investigators don't carry guns." He pulled his automatic from his holster. "But detectives do. We carry guns and every now and again, if we're lucky, we get to use them."

"Ed..." said Lumley.

"Don't worry, Joe," said Mitchell, holstering his weapon. "I wouldn't dream of accidentally putting a bullet into Mr Slater's head."

"See there's the thing, Sergeant Mitchell," said Slater, taking his pack of cigarettes from his pocket.

"You can't smoke in here, " said Lumley.

"I'm not smoking. I just want to hold the pack. It's a tactile thing." He put the pack on the table and began turning it around slowly. Side. Top. Bottom. Side. "Like I was saying, Sergeant Mitchell. It's not CSI, it's CSU. But ninety per cent of people would think it's the latter because they watch the TV show. And most people think CSI investigators carry guns and solve crimes when in fact all they do is process crime scenes."

"Your point being?" said Mitchell.

"My point being that you're telling me not to believe what I see on TV, yet you seem hell bent on believing what I wrote in a work of fiction. A novel."

"It's not the same thing at all," said Mitchell.

Slater shrugged and continued to play with the pack.

"You said you were going to kill a student," said Mitchell. "Now Jenny Cameron has disappeared and her bathroom is awash with blood."

"But no body, right?"

Mitchell narrowed his eyes. "Why do you say that?"

"Because you haven't mentioned a body. Just the blood. So all you have at the moment is a missing person who might have cut her finger."

"There was a lot of blood," said Lumley. "But you know that. You were there. You did it."

"I don't even know where Jenny lives," said Slater.

"You never went to her apartment?"

Slater shook his head. "She said she lived in Chelsea but that's all I know."

"In your book you said you followed her to her apartment."

"My book's a work of fiction."

Mitchell's eyes hardened. "What did you do with the body, Slater?"

Slater sat back in his chair and folded his arms and said nothing.

Mitchell leaned forward. "Cat got your tongue?"

Slater smiled. "See, I've never understood what that meant? How could a cat possibly have my tongue? In the whole history of emergency room medicine has a patient ever turned up with his tongue missing and blamed a cat?" He toyed with his cigarette pack as he spoke.

"You're good at avoiding answering questions that make you uncomfortable, aren't you?" said Mitchell. "Where is Jenny Cameron's body?"

"You tell me," said Slater. "And we've already agreed that all you have is blood on the floor."

"Where else could that have come from?"

Slater shrugged carelessly. "Maybe it was the wrong time of the month."

"You bastard," hissed Mitchell. He grabbed the pack, dropped it onto the floor, and stamped on it. "I've just about had as much as I can take from you."

Lumley pulled back the empty chair and sat down next to Mitchell. "How about a coffee, Adrian?" she asked. "I could do with a coffee. What about you?"

"Coffee would be good," said Slater.

"How do you take it?"

"Same as my women," said Slater. "Hot and black." He grinned. "Joke."

Lumley looked across at Mitchell. They exchanged a look and Slater realized that she wanted to be alone with him. Or at least to have Mitchell out of the room for a few minutes. He resisted the urge to smile. She wanted to play Good Cop, Bad Cop. He crossed his legs at the ankles and waited to see how she'd play it.

Mitchell left the room and Lumley waited for the door to close before speaking. When she did her voice was low and soothing, the way you'd talk to a spooked horse.

"I can see how it could've happened, Adrian. You were arguing. You lost your temper. It happens. It happens to everybody." She leaned over the table towards him, like a priest waiting to hear confession. "You lashed out, maybe she fell, hit her head. You didn't mean to do it. It just happened."

Slater put his head in his hands and muttered incoherently.

"So she's dead. It's not your fault, maybe she even asked for it. But then you panicked. That's when you remembered the book. That's what gave you the idea of getting rid of the body. So you did what anyone else would do. You got rid of the evidence. I can understand that, Adrian. She was dead. It didn't hurt her. But you have to tell us where the body is. You have to help us so that we can get you out of this mess."

Slater shook his head and mumbled something.

Lumley leaned closer. Her face was inches from his. "You can tell me, Adrian. I'm here to help you."

Slater turned his face slowly towards her, then before she could react he licked her cheek. She jumped back and yelped. Her chair fell backwards as she stood up, her eyes blazing. "If you don't start answering some questions, I'm gonna beat the living shit outta you," she shouted.

Slater leaned back and put his hands behind his head. "I'm shaking," he said.

"You think I'm joking, Slater? You think I can't do it? You think because I'm a woman I can't take you? Because you're wrong. Dead wrong."

The door opened and Mitchell walked in with three coffees on a plastic tray. "What's wrong?" he asked Lumley.

Lumley picked up the chair. "Nothing," she said.

"Detective Lumley was just explaining how investigations are carried out here in New York City," said Slater. He reached over and took one of the coffees. "You didn't spit in it, did you?" asked Slater.

"Nah," said Mitchell. "I pissed in it, though."

"Nice," said Slater. He sipped his coffee and smacked his lips appreciatively.

Mitchell sat down. "You think you're pretty darn smart, don't you?"

Slater shrugged. "I've got a pretty high IQ, that's true."

"Through the roof, I'm told." Mitchell sipped his coffee.

Slater did the same. They put their cups down on the table together. "Told by whom?"

"The therapist who treated you in Los Angeles after your father killed himself."

Slater smiled thinly. "I'm confused, Sergeant. Wouldn't my sessions with a medical professional be covered by privilege?"

"Probably," said Mitchell. "And we probably wouldn't be able to use them in court. But all we're doing here is talking. Chewing the fat."

"You spoke to my therapist?"

"Let's just say that I know that you were a bright kid but that you had issues. Bed-wetting. A few pets that got hurt. The odd fire. All the common or garden precursors of a serial killer. And that was before your father blew his head off with a shotgun."

"You're treading on dangerous ground, Mitchell," said Slater, quietly.

"Compared with what? Killing a girl and butchering her?"

"You've no proof of that. Don't you get what's happening here? The accusations you're making are pure fiction. The same as my book."

"You think this is a game, don't you?" said Mitchell.

"If it is, you're not making a very good job of it." He looked at his watch. "Time's a wasting," he said. "And as much as I enjoy these little chats. I do have a book to write."

"We've not finished," said Mitchell.

Slater stood up. "Yes you have," he said. "You've no body and no evidence. You've got nothing. If you had anything you'd have charged me already. It's time to put up or shut up, Sergeant. Either you arrest me or I'm out of here." Mitchell and Lumley looked at each other but said nothing. Slater grinned, knowing that he'd won. He threw them a mock salute. "You guys have a great day, what's left of it," he said, and walked out of the room.

Mitchell cursed and slapped his hand down on the table.

"Well that went well," said Lumley.

"We'll get the bastard," said Mitchell. "Guys like that, they want to get caught."

"I'm not sure that's true."

"He wants to know how smart he is. That'll be his downfall. Because eventually there's only one way that he can prove to us how smart he is and that's to confess."

Lumley sipped her coffee. "I'd prefer we got him by old-fashioned police work," she said.

"That'd be nice," said Mitchell. "Any thoughts on how the hell we're going to do that?"

"My thinking cap's on," she said. "Did you see the mirroring, by the way?"

"The what?"

"The mirroring. He was doing it to you all the time. When you reached for your coffee, he did. When you folded your arms, he copied you. He was even matching his breathing to yours."

"Why the hell would he do that?"

"To put you at ease."

Mitchell scowled. "Well that sure as hell didn't work, did it?"

"It's something sociopaths do, instinctively. Good salesmen do it, as well, you make a customer feel that you're in synch with him and he's more likely to do business with you. Sociopaths do it so that you'll think they're normal, when of course they're not." She nodded at the door. "Slater's a Grade A sociopath, Ed. No question of it. He's never going to confess. The big question is whether he's going to kill again or if it was just a one time thing."

"And what do you think?"

Lumley grimaced. "I think Adrian Slater is one sick son of a bitch, and one murder is more than enough. I'm going to put him behind bars if it's the last thing I do."

CHAPTER 33

Dudley Grose screwed the cap back onto his fountain pen and leaned back in his chair. The words just wouldn't come. No matter how he tried he couldn't form a coherent sentence. He'd never believed in writer's block and always thought it an excuse for laziness, but for the first time in his life he understood what it involved. His mind simply wouldn't focus, and the more he tried to concentrate the more other thoughts intruded. He kept thinking about Jenny, her soft, supple body, her smooth skin, her wet mouth. He'd phoned her half a dozen times but her cell phone was off. He'd left two messages, knowing that to leave more would make him appear too needy. When he wasn't thinking about Jenny he was thinking about Slater and his infernal book. He couldn't understand why the police hadn't simply arrested him.

Grose groaned. He stood up, massaging the back of his neck, and walked over to the window. His back was hurting, and the pain had grown worse over the past three days. He'd taken painkillers but they hadn't even taken the edge off the pain and now the discomfort was constant. His wife was busy in the garden, down on her knees and working a trowel into the soil at the base of a spreading bush. Maybe it was time to leave her. Maybe he should just walk out and move into Jenny's apartment. Maybe that would help kick start his writing again. To hell with the university, to hell with everybody.

His cell phone rang and he hurried over to his desk. His face fell when he saw that it wasn't Jenny. It was Detective Lumley, he'd stored the number last time she called.

"Dr Grose, I'm afraid I have some bad news for you," she said.

"About Slater?"

"About Jenny Cameron. I'm afraid it looks as if she might have been attacked. We haven't found her body but there's a lot of blood in her apartment."

Grose began to shake. He sat down heavily as the room swam around him.

"Dr Grose?"

"Yes, I heard you," said Grose. He took a deep breath and exhaled. "I'm sorry, I'm... I can't..."

"I understand, Dr Grose. As I said, we're not a hundred per cent sure what has happened but we can't locate Miss Cameron and at the moment we're working on the assumption that she has been murdered."

"By Adrian Slater, right? Have you arrested him?"

"We don't have any evidence yet," said Lumley.

"You've got his book," said Grose. "He admitted that he followed her home. What more do you need?"

"We need physical evidence," said Lumley. "We need proof. Or a confession."

"His whole book is a confession. The bastard went and confessed before he killed her."

"Mr Grose, you can rest assured that we will get Slater. He's not going to get away with this."

"I wish I believed that," said Grose.

"There is something you can do to help us, Dr Grose. We've dusted her apartment for fingerprints and we'll be running a comparison with Slater's prints. But we need a list of anyone else who might have visited her apartment. Friends, fellow students. Could you give us a list of anyone you think has been there so that we can get their prints?"

"Of course," said Grose. "Let me ask around when I get to the university tomorrow."

Lumley ended the call and Grose put down his cell phone. He felt suddenly light headed and he took slow, deep breaths. Jenny was dead? JENNY WAS DEAD? How could it have happened? He'd told the Head of Faculty what Slater had planned, he'd told the Dean, he'd told the cops. How could she be dead? He felt his eyes fill with tears. "Oh God, Jenny," he whispered. He put his head in his hands and began to cry.

CHAPTER 34

Lumley jumped as the car door opened. She relaxed as soon as she saw it was Mitchell, juggling a Burger King bag and two Cokes. She took the bag and one of the Cokes from him and he slid into the passenger's seat. "Anything?" he asked.

Lumley shook her head as she opened the bag. "Quiet as a mouse," she said. From where they had parked in the marina car park they had a clear view of Slater's yacht. They had followed him from the station and watched as he'd gone aboard at just after eight o'clock the previous night. It was now nine o'clock in the morning.

"The Whopper's mine, I got you a cheeseburger."

Lumley took out a Whopper and handed it to Mitchell. He put his Coke in the cup-holder and took the burger.

"There's two French fries in there," he said.

Lumley took out her cheeseburger and handed him the bag. "You can have both the fries," she said. "And the onion rings."

"Diet?"

"It's breakfast, Ed," she said. "You said you were going to get breakfast. Coffee and a croissant is what I was expecting."

"And breakfast of champions is what you got," he said. He bit into his burger and sighed before chewing.

"I can practically hear your arteries hardening," she said. She unwrapped her burger, sniffed it and took a bite. It actually tasted quite good but she faked a grimace.

Mitchell slurped his Coke and then wiped the back of his mouth with his hand. "It hasn't worked, you realize that?"

"Jury's still out," said Lumley.

"Jury's come out, announced its verdict and gone home in a taxi," said Mitchell. "If he was going to dig up the body he'd have done it by now. If he even halfway believed that we knew where he'd buried the bits then he'd have to move them."

"So the fact that he's sitting on his boat as if he didn't have a care in the world means what?" asked Lumley.

"It means that he didn't do it, which I doubt," said Mitchell. "Or it means that the thing about the numbers is all crap."

"Maybe he wants us to find the body. Maybe he wants us to catch him."

"Yeah, and maybe he's got Angelina Jolie in there and she's giving him head as we speak."

Lumley's jaw dropped. "Where did that come from?" she said.

"A personal fantasy of mine," he said. "Trust me, there's no way on earth that Slater wants us to catch him." He took another bite of his Whopper.

"So does he think we won't crack the code in the book?"

"Maybe there is no code," said Mitchell through a mouthful of burger. "All you have is a load of meaningless numbers. Maybe that's all they are. Meaningless."

Lumley shook her head. "There are too many numbers in his book. They're unnecessary."

"Maybe he's just messing with your head."

Lumley frowned. "You think?"

"That's how he gets his kicks. He likes playing games. I wouldn't put it past him just throwing in numbers so that you'd jump to exactly the conclusion that you have jumped to. So no, I don't actually think he's in there getting head from Angelina Jolie but I sure as hell do think he's in there with a shit-eating grin on his face."

"But you think he did it?"

"Of course he did it." He slurped his Coke again and smacked his lips. "But if we just sit here and wait for him to lead us to the body, we'll be waiting until hell freezes over. If we're going to put him behind bars, we're going to have to do it the old-fashioned way."

"Beat a confession out of him with phone directories?"

Mitchell chuckled. "I wasn't thinking of going back that far," he said. He put the Coke into the cup-holder and pulled out his cell phone. "Did you see that?" he asked, nodding at the yacht.

"See what?"

"Slater on the deck. Just then. He was holding a gun."

"What the hell are you talking about, Ed?"

"A gun. An automatic, I think it was." He started tapping out a number on his cell phone with his thumb. "The captain's got a couple of tame judges who'll be more than happy to issue a search warrant, especially as we saw the gun."

Lumley grinned. "Oh, that gun? The big one? Damn right I saw it." She took another bite of her burger as Mitchell continued to tap out the number.

CHAPTER 35

Slater was standing on the pier next to his yacht, bookended by two large uniformed cops. He was wearing a long black coat over his black jeans and had his RayBans pushed up on top of his head. "Look at him, like butter wouldn't melt in his backside," said Lumley. She was standing with Mitchell at the entrance to the marina.

"He doesn't look worried," said Mitchell. The two uniforms took Slater to a cruiser and put him in the back. They hadn't handcuffed him yet because he hadn't been arrested.

"He's a psychopath," said Lumley. "They're expert at hiding their feelings."

"Either that or there's nothing on the boat."

"Oh ye of little faith," said Lumley. She punched him lightly on the shoulder. "Come on, let's see how they're getting on."

They walked along the pier and boarded the yacht at the rear. There were two CSU technicians in the main cabin and a third was in the sleeping cabin at the front of the boat.

"How's it going?" Lumley asked the technician closest to the hatch. She was a red-head with high cheekbones and a sprinkling of freckles across her nose. Like the rest of the technicians she was wearing a white paper suit and had blue paper covers over her shoes. She had just finished spraying luminol over the floor and was sitting back on her heels to see if there was any reaction.

"Nothing," said the technician. "I've done the shower and the galley and there's no blood anywhere." She nodded at the technician in the forward cabin. "We're checking the sheets for whatever, but again there's no blood. We did find blonde hairs in a hairbrush in the head so we'll run them against hairs from the girl's apartment. And there are lots of fingerprints."

The technician pointed at a large textbook on the desk next to a laptop. "You might want to look at the book," she said. "And that roll thing. That's very interesting. It's a chef's knife set. Professional, too. Japanese. Those blades will cut right through bone." The technician grinned mischievously. "And you might want to look at the notepad, too."

Lumley picked up the notepad and grimaced when she saw the caricature that Slater had drawn. He'd sketched her and Mitchell as Keystone cops, waving truncheons as they chased after Slater on his motorcycle. She showed it to Mitchell and he shook his head. "We need the knives checked for blood," he told the technician.

"We'll do that at the lab," said the technician. "But I have to tell you they look like they've been thoroughly cleaned and there's a strong smell of bleach on them." She headed into the sleeping area to talk to the other technician.

Mitchell picked up the book. Gray's Dissection Guide For Human Anatomy. "Now why would a writer need that?" he said.

"He'll say it's for research," said Lumley, tossing the notepad onto the desk.

"It's a guide to dismembering a body," said Mitchell. "That and the knives does it for me."

"But it won't do it for a judge, or a jury," said Lumley. She switched on the laptop.

"I hate to be the stickler for the rules but the warrant doesn't cover his computer," said Mitchell. "We're looking for the gun we saw and at a stretch that can be used to cover the knives, but the laptop is out of reach."

Lumley grinned and took out a small black thumbdrive from her pocket. "I don't want the laptop," she said. "I just want a look-see at his work in progress, see how much further he's got."

"Naughty girl," said Mitchell, standing so that his body was between her and the technicians.

"By hook or by crook, we're going to get this bastard," said Lumley. She plugged the thumbdrive into the laptop's USB slot, found the work in progress file and copied it. It took her less than a minute, then she pocketed the thumbdrive and switched off the laptop.

They went up the stairs to the deck. Slater was looking at them from the back of the cruiser. He blew Lumley a kiss.

Mitchell scowled. "He knows there's nothing here to hurt him," he said. "The boat's clean. He isn't going to confess. There's no body. We're screwed, no matter which way you look at it."

"Not if we find the body," said Lumley. "I need to solve the clues in the book."

"We're not sure there are clues to be solved."

"There are, Ed. I'm sure of it. Slater wants to prove that he's smarter than us. He wants to shove his intelligence in our faces, rub our noses in it." She forced a smile. "Come on, let's go. I want to go through the latest version of his book. And this time I'm going to get an expert to help me."

"An expert?"

"A mathematician, someone who's good with numbers. If the clues are in that book, I need someone who can point me in the right direction," she said.

CHAPTER 36

Lumley didn't know any mathematicians. In fact she didn't know anyone, family or friends, who could even balance their own checkbook. But she did know how to use Google and within minutes at her computer she had the email addresses of half a dozen mathematicians who worked in New York City. She sent the same short email to all six and by the end of her shift she had received replies from four. All were intrigued and the following day she visited them one by one and left them thumbdrives containing Slater's book.

All were male, all were in their thirties and all had facial hair, though one of them was bald and another had hair that had receded halfway across his scalp. All four wore glasses and all seemed to have trouble looking her in the eyes. Three were Doctors and the fourth was a consultant whose clients included the IRS, the ATF and the FBI. His name was Alex Brennan and he seemed the most normal of the four. He wore a dark grey suit and a tie and there was a photograph of a chubby blonde woman and three equally chubby children on his desk. His office was several floors below the FBI's field office in Federal Plaza and on the wall behind him were framed commendations and plaques from police forces around the country. He had polished his horn-rimmed spectacles as he listened to Lumley and had nodded enthusiastically while looking out of the window. When she gave him the thumbdrive she'd noticed that his nails were bitten to the quick.

It was Brennan who got back to her first, just twenty-four hours later, to announce that he'd cracked the code. Cracked it and come up with three locations already. All of them in New York.

CHAPTER 37

Mitchell and Lumley picked up Slater at eight o'clock in the morning, handcuffed him and drove him to the police station. They didn't say anything to him and he didn't attempt to initiate a conversation. They took him straight to an interview room where Lumley took off the cuffs and told him to sit down. "Why so serious, Detective Lumley?" asked Slater.

"It's over, Slater," she said, sitting down opposite him. "Your sick, evil little game has come to an end. And now it's time for you to pay the piper."

Mitchell sat down next to her.

Slater took out his cigarettes. "Can I smoke?"

"It's a public building, of course you can't fucking smoke," said Lumley.

"It relaxes me. Nicotine is my drug of choice and smoking apart it's not illegal. Depriving me of my nicotine is against my human rights, surely."

"It's against the law," said Lumley.

Slater put the cigarettes away and folded his arms. "So what is this, Good Cop and Stupid Cop?" he said. "It's not a combination I've come across before. Does it usually work for you?"

"Did you kill Jenny Cameron?" asked Mitchell.

"Is that what passes for interrogation in New York City?" said Slater. "How do you think I'm going to answer a question like that?" He held out his hands. "You got me, Detective Mitchell. I confess. Lock me up and throw away the key, why don't you?"

Mitchell pointed a finger at Slater. "You've got a very funny mouth, Slater," he growled.

"Yeah, but you can't charge me with that, can you." He looked at his watch. "And if I'm not charged then I can go whenever I want to. So are we done? Or do you have some more insightful questions to get me quivering in my boots?"

"Do you know where Jenny Cameron is?" asked Lumley.

"Why would I? I'm not her father."

"But you are her lover, right?" said Mitchell.

"See, now you're getting your tenses all mixed up," said Slater. "If she's dead then I can't be her lover in the present tense. You are saying she's dead, right?"

"You don't seem surprised," said Mitchell. "Or sorry."

"Because I'm confused," said Slater. "And the reason I'm confused is because your line of questioning is so random."

"How do you explain her disappearance?"

Slater shrugged. "She wasn't doing well on the course. Maybe she realized that she wasn't cut out to be a writer and went home."

"We checked with her parents," said Lumley. "She hasn't gone home. They haven't heard from her in two weeks."

"Her fingerprints were on the boat," said Mitchell. "And we found hairs on a brush with her DNA. Perfect match to the DNA in the blood we found in her bathroom. And we found epithelials on your sheets."

Slater frowned. "Epithelials? You mean skin cells?"

"Jenny Cameron's skin. She was in your bed."

"So?"

"You were lovers?"

"I wouldn't say that."

"What would you say?" asked Mitchell.

"Friends."

"Friends with benefits?" said Lumley.

"Just friends," said Slater.

"You never had sex with her?" asked Mitchell.

"She came on the boat. She felt a bit queasy. She lay down for a bit. She left. There was no sex involved. I took her sailing. We had some wine. We watched the sun go down. Yada yada yada."

"Yada, yada, yada?"

"Yeah. It means nothing happened."

The two detectives looked at Slater for several seconds without saying anything.

"The silent treatment?" said Slater. "That's not going to work either."

"You ever hear about a book called Masquerade?" asked Lumley.

Slater shrugged. "It doesn't ring a bell."

"You sure about that?"

"What is it? A thriller?"

"No. Definitely not a thriller."

"There was a movie called Masquerade, right? With Rob Lowe?"

"This was a book. By an English guy, Kit Williams. It was a sort of fairy story, but there were clues in it that would lead the reader to find some hidden treasure."

"You've lost me, Detective. Sorry." Slater sat back in his chair and folded his arms.

"The book was based around a series of fifteen paintings. In the paintings were clues that pointed to the location of a golden hare. Hare as in a rabbit."

"I'm still not following you," said Slater.

"It was published in 1979. Huge fanfare, I'm told. People all over the world bought the book and started looking for the treasure. The golden hare was worth tens of thousands of dollars and treasure hunters started digging holes all over the place."

"Sounds like a good way of boosting sales, what do you think, Mr Slater?" asked Mitchell.

Slater shrugged but didn't say anything.

"So you never heard of this book?" asked Lumley.

"Like I said, it doesn't ring a bell," said Slater.

"Because it got me thinking, about your book. The Bestseller. There are lots of numbers in it."

"There's some."

"No, there's a lot. Phone numbers, apartment numbers, zip codes, car registration numbers. More than you'd normally find in a novel."

"I'm not sure that's true."

Lumley nodded. "Oh, it's true. Lots of numbers. And that got me thinking. Maybe the numbers are there for a reason."

Slater's jaw tensed and his eyes hardened. His right hand clenched into a tight fist.

"You see, we were going about it the wrong way. We were looking for clues in the story. I mean, you talk about choosing the victim and how you were going to kill her and dispose of the body. But the clues aren't in the words, are they? They're in the numbers."

Slater said nothing.

"And you're a sailor. Sailing is all about navigation. GPS coordinates. Latitude and longitude. It's all in the numbers isn't it? Crack the code and we'll find the body. Or the bits of it. Am I right?"

"Do you think I'm crazy, Detective Lumley? Do you think I'd cut up a body and bury the parts in some sort of crazy treasure hunt? Why would I do that?"

"The clue's in the title. The Bestseller. You want to be famous. And I think you've realized that your writing isn't good enough to get you noticed. You need a gimmick. A USP. A unique selling point."

"And you think a book that says that I'm going to kill a girl and then highlight where the body's buried is a good way to get onto the bestseller list?"

"Don't you?"

"I think it's a surefire way of ending up in jail. Or the electric chair. You've got the death penalty in New York, haven't you?"

"It's been declared unconstitutional," said Mitchell "But you never know."

"Death penalty or not, I'd be pretty stupid to tell everyone in advance what I was doing, wouldn't I?"

"You don't see it that way, though, do you?" said Lumley.

"What do you mean?"

"You think you're smarter than the rest of us. It's clear from the way you talk, your body language, everything you do, that you regard us all as intellectually inferior. Am I right?"

Slater sighed. "I'm not going to give you the satisfaction of agreeing or disagreeing," he said.

"You know what I think, Slater? I think you're a sociopath. I think you've decided that you want to be a famous writer and that you'll do whatever it takes to achieve that objective. But you're right, I don't think you're stupid enough to tell people where you buried the body parts. You weren't planning to tell anyone, were you? It was going to be your secret."

Mitchell nodded slowly. "Serial killers take trophies, you know that? They keep a little something so that they can relive the experience. A piece of jewelry, bit of clothing, a photograph maybe. But you, I think you found some other way of getting off on the murder. You left clues in the book, clues that only you would ever know about. And reading that book and knowing that the clues are there is what will get you hard."

Slater swallowed nervously and looked at the two detectives in turn. Then he slowly smiled. "Nice try," he said. "But if that was true then you'd have the body parts and we wouldn't be having this conversation."

"And you never read that book? Masquerade?"

Slater shook his head.

"That's real strange," said Mitchell. "Because your father had the film rights at one stage."

"Is that right?"

"Apparently so. He was working on a script, based on the book and the search for the hare. You'd be just a kid at the time but he'd have had a copy, for sure."

"My father didn't usually talk about his work with me."

"That doesn't sound right," said Mitchell. "Kids always want to know about their father's work."

"Yeah? Was your father a cop, Sergeant Mitchell? Did you learn interrogation techniques at his knee?"

Mitchell glared at Slater but before he could reply, Lumley began to speak. "We're giving you the opportunity of putting an end to this," she said. "Let Jenny's parents have her body so that they can give her a proper burial. And we can get you the treatment you need."

"Since when have cops cared about treating people?"

"You're sick, Adrian. You know you're sick. You can't control yourself and you're going to keep killing until you get caught. It'll go a lot easier for you if you put an end to it now."

Slater nodded slowly as he stared at the detective. "How do you know so much about it?"

"You're not the first person we've had in here with your problem, Adrian."

"Is that what it is, a problem?"

"It's not normal, is it?" said Lumley. "You know that. That's why you need help. And we can help you. If you cooperate with us now we'll be in your corner. We'll do what we can to make things easier for you. But if you fight us, we'll take you down and we'll take you down hard. Do you understand?"

Slater nodded.

Lumley reached over and patted the back of his hand. "So tell us, Adrian. Tell us where the body is so that we can bring this to an end. We need closure. And so do you."

Slater looked at Lumley, then turned to look at Mitchell. Mitchell was holding his breath as he stared expectantly at Slater.

"There's one thing you can do for me, Joe," said Slater, his voice hardly more than a whisper.

"What?" she asked.

He turned his hands over and held her by the wrists. "A blow job," he said. "Give me a blow job and I'll give you closure, all over your pretty little lips."

Lumley tried to pull away from him but he tightened his grip.

"You bastard!" she shouted.

Mitchell stood up so quickly that his chair fell back and hit the ground with the sound of a gunshot.

Slater grinned at Lumley. "Come on, Joe, you know you want to."

Mitchell grabbed Slater by his shirt and pulled him to his feet. Lumley pushed her chair back, a look of disgust on her face. Mitchell drew back his fist and Slater's grin widened.

Mitchell's fist began to shake as he struggled with himself.

"Go on, Ed, you can do it," said Slater. "You know you want to."

Mitchell roared and pushed Slater back. Slater stumbled over his chair and fell to the floor. His head banged against the wall and he lay still.

"Ed!" shouted Lumley. She stood up and went over to the Sergeant. "What have you done?"

"He fell," said Mitchell.

She looked down at Slater. "He hit his head. Ed, you could have killed him."

"He's playing possum," said Mitchell. He bent down and shook Slater's shoulder. "He assaulted you. He grabbed you and made an indecent suggestion."

"He's not moving, Ed."

Mitchell shook Slater again. His eyes were closed and Mitchell couldn't see his chest moving. He knelt down and felt for a pulse in Slater's neck.

"Should I call for a medic?" asked Lumley.

"A lawyer would be more use," said Slater, opening his eyes. Mitchell pulled back his hand as if he'd been stung. "Gotcha," grinned Slater. "Can I go now? Or do we get a lawyer in here and show him my bruises? I'm easy either way."

Lumley's cell phone rang and she took the call. She listened intently, and then a smile slowly spread across her face. She put the phone away and pointed a finger at Slater. "Game over," she said. "We've got you."

CHAPTER 38

They handcuffed Slater and drove him to Central Park. There was a police cruiser waiting for them along with a van from the police academy and a CSU vehicle, parked with its lights flashing. An overweight uniformed cop pointed them in the right direction and they headed off across the park, Mitchell and Lumley walking either side of Slater.

"How about taking the cuffs off so that I can have a cigarette?" he asked.

"It's illegal to smoke in the park," growled Mitchell.

"You know why we're here, don't you?" said Lumley.

"To get a breath of fresh air," said Slater.

"To put you behind bars," said Lumley.

Ahead of them were a group of police cadets in blue overalls holding shovels and pickaxes. They had stopped digging and had moved away from the area of grass that they'd been working on. A CSU investigator was photographing something in the ground while two uniformed officers looked on.

A second CSU investigator walked over, holding a portable GPS unit. He was in his late twenties with a shock of ginger hair and freckles across an upturned nose. "Detective Lumley?" he said.

She nodded. "What have you found?" she asked.

"A leg," he said. "Part of a leg, anyway. From the hip to the knee."

Lumley looked at Slater. "Got anything to say now?"

Slater shrugged.

"Come on Slater. We got this location from your book. We cracked your code. We've got another four teams digging at the moment and before long we'll have them all."

Lumley's cell phone rang and she walked away from Slater to take the call.

"You know you're done for, don't you?" Mitchell said to him. "You think you're so clever but you're not half as smart as you think you are."

Slater grinned. "Let's wait until the fat lady's sung, shall we, Sergeant Mitchell?"

Lumley walked back, putting her phone away. "We've got an arm in Battery Park," she said. "Complete with a charm bracelet that we know Jenny used to wear. You're about to be charged with murder, Slater."

CHAPTER 39

The Medical Examiner looked down at the body parts on the metal table and shook his head. "What sort of sick bastard would do something like this?" he asked. He had a name badge identifying him as Darren Wilmot. He was a large black man with a shaved head and a boxer's broken nose and he was wearing pale green surgical scrubs.

"A psycho who wants to be famous," said Mitchell.

"Is he a butcher, because he's done a professional job," said Wilmot.

There was a thigh, a left foot, a right shin, one forearm, two hands, and a section of torso laid so more than half of the body was still missing.

"He had a book on dissection and some very sharp knives," said Lumley.

"No sign of the head?"

"We're working on it," said Lumley.

"Did you know she was pregnant?" asked Wilmot, looking at his notes which were clipped to a stainless steel clipboard.

"We didn't," said Lumley. "Can you get DNA so that we can identify the father?"

"I'll have it for you by tomorrow. So what's the story, I was told he was hiding the body parts all over the city? Why would he do that?"

"Like I said, he's a psycho," said Mitchell. "But we've got him, so all's well that ends well."

"Didn't end so well for the girl or her baby, did it?" said Wilmot.

Lumley's cell phone rang. "Might be another body part," she said, and took the call. It wasn't a CSU calling it was her captain, and she wanted her in the office, right away. "Is there a problem, ma'am?" she asked.

"Just get back here pronto, and make sure Mitchell comes with you," growled the captain and she cut the connection.

"Problems?" asked Mitchell.

"Not sure," said Lumley.

CHAPTER 40

Captain Chantal Kawczynski scowled at Mitchell and Lumley and pressed the stop button on the digital recorder. "Do you need to hear that again?" she asked.

"No, Ma'am," said Mitchell.

"When did the call come in?" asked Lumley.

"Three days ago to the Crime Stoppers hotline. The call came from an unregistered cell phone that at the moment is switched off."

"And why are we only just getting to hear of it now?" asked Lumley.

"You heard the caller. A middle-aged man carrying parcels into a car in the middle of the night in upstate New York. One of the parcels looked like it might be an arm. A description of a car and a plate number. It's taken time to work through the system."

"And that car is registered to Dudley Grose?" said Mitchell.

"It's in his wife's name," said the captain. She pushed her black-framed spectacles higher up her nose. "Now you tell me what's going on. We've got Adrian Slater downstairs charged with the murder of Jenny Cameron. And we're saying that he dismembered the girl and distributed the body parts around the State."

"He did it, ma'am, we're sure of that."

"That's as may be, detective, but now we've got a call saying that a man who matches the description of the girl's lecturer was seen acting suspiciously just after she vanished. At the very least we need to check that vehicle. Get a CSU unit out there ASAP."

"Yes ma'am," said Mitchell.

"And if it looks like we've got the wrong man in custody, you let me know straight away. The last thing we need is a lawsuit."

"There's no mistake, ma'am," said Lumley. "Slater did it. I'd stake my job on it."

"Detective, you might well be doing just that," said Kawczynski.

CHAPTER 41

Dudley Grose looked over his shoulder at the two heavyset uniformed police officers standing at the front door to his house. He put his arm around his wife who was looking anxiously up at him. "I don't understand why we can't go into the house," he said.

A CSU with a flashlight was peering into the rear of Grose's SUV, which was parked in front of the house. "We have a warrant to search your vehicle," said Lumley. "But if we find anything we might want to extend the warrant to cover your house, so until we know for sure we're going to need you and your wife to stay outside."

"Dudley, what's this about?" asked Mrs Grose.

"I don't know, honey. They won't say." He smiled at Lumley. "Look, can't you at least tell us what it is you're looking for. It's clearly a mistake, and if I knew what you wanted I'm sure we could get this resolved without the need for all this fuss."

"It won't take us long," said Mitchell.

"Is it Slater? Did he say something? Is he accusing me of something?"

"Who's Slater?" asked Mrs Grose, but her husband ignored her.

"It is, isn't it? That bastard Slater has accused me of something, hasn't he?"

"Let's just get the back of the car checked out," said Lumley. "If it's clean then we'll apologise and we'll be on our way."

"And my lawyer will be all over you like a rash," said Grose. "You can't do this."

Mitchell nodded at the warrant in Grose's hand. "With that we can, Mr Grose. Now please, just bear with us."

"Detectives!" called the CSU technician. "Could you come over here please?"

Mitchell hurried over to the car and Lumley followed.

"There are traces of blood," said the CSU technician. He was Hispanic, young and good looking and he made a point of addressing Lumley rather than Mitchell. "Definitely human. I'll be able to carry out the DNA analysis when I get back to the lab."

"Show me," said Mitchell.

The CSU investigator showed him a small smear on the underside of one of the seats, and a cent-sized drop close to the door locking mechanism.

"Let's get that warrant extended," Mitchell said to Lumley. "We need to look inside the house. And garden."

"There's something else," said the technician. He held out his right hand. Sitting in the middle of his gloved palm was a small gold charm. A cat.

CHAPTER 42

Dudley Grose slumped forward and banged his head on the table, the dull thuds echoing around the interview room. "Please stop doing that, Dr Grose," said Lumley. "You're not helping yourself."

Grose stayed where he was with his forehead against the table. "Why won't you just listen to me?" he said. "I didn't kill her. Why would I kill her?"

"We found traces of Jenny's blood in your car, Dr Grose, can you explain that?"

"Slater must have put it there."

"And we found a gold charm that we know used to be on her charm bracelet."

"He must have put that there too."

"And there was dirt on your tires that matched soil at Battery Park where we found one of the body parts. Does Adrian Slater have access to your vehicle?"

"Maybe my wife left the rear door open. He was in my house, remember? Maybe he got a copy of the key. How do I know?"

Mitchell reached into a black holdall and took out a carving knife in a plastic evidence bag. "Do you recognize this, Dr Grose?"

Grose sat up and blinked at the knife. "I don't know," he said. "Maybe."

"Maybe?" said Mitchell. "Do you or don't you?"

"It looks like the knives we have in our kitchen. But I don't know. How would I know? Who looks at their kitchen utensils?"

"We found this knife buried in your garden, Dr Grose. Under a bush."

"That's impossible."

"I can show you photographs of the knife being dug up," said Mitchell. "I can also tell you that although the knife had been wiped clean, we found traces of Jenny Cameron's blood and your DNA on it."

"If the knife is from my kitchen, of course it would have my DNA on it. But I wouldn't bury it in the garden, would I?"

"And how do you explain the blood on the knife?" pressed Mitchell.

"Slater," said Grose. "He must have put it there. Maybe he took it when he was in my house. Remember I reported it and you said there was nothing you could do."

"And I can also tell you that we have matched this knife to marks on the various bones that we have so far uncovered and there is no doubt that it was used to dismember Jenny Cameron's body."

"It wasn't me," said Grose. "Why would I kill her? I loved her."

"If you loved her, why didn't you leave your wife?" asked Lumley. She stood and went to stand by the door, folding her arms. "We've spoken to your wife, she said that you'd never discussed divorce. As far as she's concerned your marriage was just fine. A little stale, perhaps, but she had no reason to think you were going to leave her."

"It was complicated," said Grose. "If I'd moved in with Jenny I'd have lost everything. My house, my job." He shrugged. "I wanted to, but I couldn't bring myself to do it."

"Because your job was important to you?" asked Lumley.

"Of course. Without my job I have no money, no health benefits, I'd have nothing."

"And at fifty-two, that wouldn't be a good position to be in, would it?"

"I assume that question is rhetorical," said Grose. "Look, I loved Jenny. In a way, I still love my wife. If I'd been more of a man then yes I should have left my wife and moved in with Jenny. But I didn't. But that sure as hell doesn't give me a reason to want her dead."

"If Jenny had told the Faculty about your relationship, you'd have lost your job, wouldn't you?" said Lumley.

"Perhaps," said Grose. "But she wouldn't do that. She wasn't that sort of person. She wasn't vindictive."

Lumley walked back to the table and sat down. Grose ran his hands through his hair and cursed.

"Dudley, look at me," said Lumley quietly.

Grose put his hands down on the table and took a deep breath. "I did not kill Jenny Cameron," he said.

"Dudley, did she tell you she was pregnant?"

The color drained from Grose's face. "What?"

"She was carrying your baby. The DNA proves it was yours. She was eight weeks pregnant."

Grose slumped in his chair and covered his face with his hands. He began to sob quietly.

"Did you know?" asked Lumley, her voice little more than a whisper. "Did she tell you she was pregnant?"

Grose looked up, blinking away tears. "Is that what you think? You think I killed her because she was having my baby?"

"I think that you killed her because if it became known that you'd made a student pregnant you'd lose your wife and your job. And probably never sell another book." Grose shook his head and closed his eyes. "So you read Slater's manuscript and thought maybe you could use that to put the blame on him. You cracked the code, some of it anyway. You killed Jenny and you buried the body parts in the places that Slater's book described. You knew that Slater would be the obvious suspect. You just didn't plan on being seen."

Grose wiped his eyes with the back of his hand. "Seen? By who?"

"Someone dropped a dime on you," said Mitchell. "A woman saw you putting the body parts into your car."

"What woman?"

"Just a woman. She phoned it in."

"Who is she?" asked Grose.

"It was anonymous," said Lumley. "But anonymous or not, we've got all the evidence we need."

"Slater made that call," said Grose.

"It was a woman," said Mitchell.

"Are you stupid?" hissed Grose. "Slater got her to call. It's been Slater right from the start. Don't you see?" He began to sob again.

"Are you prepared to give us a statement, Dudley?" asked Lumley. She pushed a yellow pad and a ballpoint pen across the table towards him. "You're a writer, Dudley. Why not put it down in writing?"

"I want to be on my own," said Grose. "I need to think. I need to get my head straight."

Mitchell looked across at Lumley. "Let's let Dr Grose have a few minutes to himself. I'm sure he'll realize that the best thing to do is to tell us exactly what happened."

"Can we get you a coffee, Dr Grose?" asked Lumley. "Or water?"

Grose nodded. "Water, please." He sniffed and wiped his eyes.

The two detectives left the room and stood in the corridor. "What do you think?" asked Lumley.

"I think he's going to confess," said Mitchell. "Look at the tears. He's sorry. He's going to have to get it off his chest, sooner or later."

Lumley folded her arms. "And we're sure, we're sure that he did it?"

"What's the alternative? You think Slater could have set the whole thing up? Look at the evidence, Joe. We've got him on a plate."

Lumley nodded. "I guess so."

"Let's see what Grose says after he's had time to get his thoughts together. My bet is that he'll tell us everything. If he doesn't, okay, we can have another look at Slater. But my money is on the cry baby in there."

CHAPTER 43

Grose sat with his head in his hands. His life was over. Finished. He hadn't killed Jenny but that didn't matter. There was a chance that a jury might believe he was innocent, but that didn't matter either. Even if he could convince a jury that he hadn't killer her, she had been his lover and she had been carrying his baby. They were facts, and they were facts that Karen would never forgive. Neither would the university. And neither would his readers, the few that he had left. The tabloids would have a field day. Lecturer murders pregnant student lover.

He'd need a top legal team and that would cost money. Serious money. Probably every penny that he had. And Karen wouldn't forgive his infidelity, especially when she discovered that Jenny had been carrying his baby. She'd never forgive him for that, not after all the years that she'd tried so hard to bear a child. She'd divorce him, he was sure of that. He'd lose the house, and she'd take whatever money he had left after paying his lawyers. Guilty or innocent he'd lose his job. The University had a zero tolerance policy when it came to staff getting involved with students. And no other educational establishment in the country would hire him.

Grose groaned like an animal in pain. He'd never be published again, no matter what the result of the trial. Even if he managed to avoid the murder charge, no one was going to publish a book by a lecturer who got a student pregnant, a student who was then brutally killed and her body dismembered. No one would remember his Pulitzer nomination, or the glowing reviews of Snow Birds, the awards that he'd won and the lectures that he'd given. All anyone would care about is that he was Dudley Grose, the dirty old man. The pervert. He began to sob and tears rolled down his cheeks. His life was over. No matter what happened, he was finished. Worst possible scenario he'd spend the rest of his life behind bars. Best possible scenario he'd be penniless, homeless and alone. He wasn't sure which was worse, but he knew one thing for sure – he couldn't face either scenario. He would be better off dead.

He sat up straight and wiped the tears from his eyes. He didn't have long, they still hadn't charged him so they hadn't searched him and taken away his belongings. He patted his pockets down and smiled to himself when he felt the hardness of the pen in the top inside pocket of his jacket. He took it out slowly. It was his black Mont Blanc, a gift from his wife. He held the pen in his right hand and brushed it against his cheek. She'd given it to him on their wedding day. He'd replaced the nib countless times over the years and had fitted a new one only three weeks earlier.

He took a deep breath, and then wiped his nose with the back of his left hand. He wanted to leave a note, but he knew that there wasn't time. To say what he wanted to say would take too long, require too much thought. There was so much he had to say. Regret, of course. Regret for betraying his wife. Regret for not spending more time writing and less time fooling around with a girl young enough to be his daughter. Grose felt his cheeks redden with shame. What had he been thinking? When he first started talking to Jenny as anything more than a teacher addressing his student, what the hell had been going through his mind? There was anger too, and he'd need time to express that anger properly, time that he didn't have. He wanted to blame Slater, because he was sure that it was Slater who had killed Jenny, killed her and framed Grose for the murder. But even more he wanted to blame Dean Martin and the Head of Faculty. They had forced the course on to him, and they had refused to back him up once it became clear that Slater was becoming a problem. If they had simply shown Slater the door when Grose had first raised the matter then none of this would have happened.

Jenny wouldn't have been murdered and Grose wouldn't have been.... He shuddered. There was no point in thinking about what might have been. The past was the past, dwelling on it wouldn't achieve anything. All that mattered now was the situation that he was in, and how he dealt with it.

He slowly unscrewed the cap off the pen and placed it on the bunk beside him. The gold nib glinted under the fluorescent light overhead. He stared at the pen and smiled at the irony of it. He'd lived to write, his whole life that was the only thing that he'd wanted to do, and so it was only fitting that it should be a pen that ended it. He took another deep breath and exhaled slowly as he prepared himself to do what had to be done. It would hurt, he knew that, but it wouldn't hurt for long. He gripped the pen tightly with his right hand, so tightly that his knuckles whitened. He pressed the nib against the flesh, about two inches below the wrist, close to where a thick blue vein branched into two. He looked up at the ceiling and then closed his eyes. He gasped as he pushed the pen hard and then twisted so that the gold nib tore through the skin. He bit down on his lower lip, twisted the pen and pushed harder as blood gushed over his hand.

CHAPTER 44

ONE YEAR LATER

The line ran for a hundred yards outside the book store, threading its way past the front of Rite-Aid and Burger King and a beauty parlor and an office supplies store and down the road and around the corner. The line went through the front door of the book store, up a flight of stairs and ended at a large desk which was piled high with hardback copies of a book. THE BESTSELLER. The cover was jet black with a gleaming stainless steel knife in the center, its tip bloody. Above the blade was the title and below it the name of the author. ADRIAN SLATER.

Slater was grinning as he signed a copy of his book with a flourish and passed it to the pretty brunette on the other side of the desk. "I hope you enjoy it," he said. He was wearing a black Armani suit and a grey shirt and a gold Rolex glinted on his wrist.

"Oh I'm sure I will," she gushed. "I saw you on The Tonight Show and Jay Leno made it sound so good. Are you doing a sequel?"

"I'm planning one as we speak," said Slater.

One of the glossy PR girls that the publisher had sent to help organize the signing gently led the brunette away. The next buyer stepped up to the desk and Slater took a book off the pile at his elbow. "Who shall I make it out to," he said for the hundredth time. He looked up and then did a double-take as he recognized the girl standing in front of him.

She smiled. "Kirsty," she said. "And maybe you could write "with love" or something like that. Make it more personal."

She was wearing her hair long and as he stared up at her she slowly tilted her head to the right and brushed her hair over her left ear, revealing a thick rope-like scar across her neck. There were scars on her hand, too, deep cuts that had healed badly.

"It's a great book," she said. "I read it as soon as it came out. I'd pre-ordered it on Amazon."

"They provide a great service," said Slater. He started to sign the book but his hand trembled and he took a deep breath, trying to steady himself.

"There's no need to be nervous, Adrian," said Kirsty, dipping her head and allowing her hair to fall back to cover the scar.

A PR girl reached out to touch Kirsty's arm but Kirsty shook her away. "I'm an old friend. Tell her Adrian. Tell her I'm an old friend."

Adrian nodded at the PR girl. "I know her," he said. "Just give us a minute."

The PR girl flashed him a professional smile but he could see that she wasn't happy. "Let's get a coffee later," Slater said to Kirsty.

"A coffee would be nice," she said.

"Cool," said Slater. He scrawled "For Kirsty, With Love" across a page and underneath it scrawled a lazy signature. He closed the book and handed it to her, but she didn't take it.

"It's everything you said it would be," she said.

"I'm glad you enjoyed it." He offered her the book but she stood with her hands holding the strap of her shoulder bag.

"I didn't say that I enjoyed it, Adrian. I said that it was everything that you said it would be. A true bestseller. Not quite the same as the version I saw back in LA, but a gripping read. And the plot twist where it turns out that the lecturer is the killer. Well, I never saw that coming. That was inspired."

Slater said nothing. He swallowed and the back of his throat was so dry that he almost gagged. He put down the book and reached for a glass of water.

"Where is it in the bestseller lists? Number seven?"

Slater took a sip of water. "Six this morning."

"On the way to number one," she said. "After Leno you'll be selling a million, I'm sure."

"Hopefully," said Slater. He put down the glass. "But nothing's ever guaranteed." He looked at his wristwatch. "I'm going to have to get on with signing," he said. "There's a hundred or so in the line and I have to be out of here by two."

"I was surprised at the name. Adrian Slater. Is that a pen name?"

"No. That's me."

"So Eddie Wilson was what? A dry run? Was that what I was, Adrian? A dry run? Practice?"

"What do you want, Kirsty?" He took another sip of water and then put down the glass. His hand trembled as the glass touched the table and water slopped over the side.

Kirsty smiled. "What happened to your ePublishing idea?" she asked. "I thought you were going to bypass the publishers and sell it yourself."

"It's hard to turn down a seven-figure deal," said Slater. "And let's face it, there's nothing to compare with the feel of a real book. The smell of it. At the end of the day an eReader is just a small computer, and where's the romance in that?"

"That's so funny. In LA I was the one who said that eBooks were an abomination and that paper was all that mattered. Funny how thing's change. Like your name. Who knew that Eddie Wilson wasn't your real name? And who knew that before you were Adrian Slater you were Adrian Henderson? How's your foot, by the way?"

"It's fine."

She waved her scarred right hand in front of him. "I wasn't so lucky. Well, I suppose I was in that I didn't die. A truck driver took me to hospital but I passed out and by the time I could talk you'd long gone. I see from the book that you've still got the boat?"

Slater nodded.

"No trace of it in LA," said Kirsty. "The cops looked. Or at least they said they did. I suppose you changed the name."

"Thought it might be best."

"You know that's unlucky, don't you? Changing the name of a boat." Kirsty's eyes had gone cold. Lifeless. Like glass. "How did you get the boat from the West Coast over to New York?"

"Sailed it," said Slater. "All the way down to the Panama Canal and all the way back up again."

"Single-handed?"

"Always. It gave me time to think."

"No wonder the cops couldn't find you," she said. "Towards the end I think they stopped believing that I was attacked. One of the cops even asked me if I'd hurt myself. Can you believe that?"

"Cops are stupid," said Slater. "The world over."

"The ones in your book certainly are," said Kirsty. "Aren't you going to ask me what I'm doing with myself these days?"

Slater looked over at the two PR girls but they were deep in conversation with their backs to him. He looked back at Kirsty and forced a smile. "Okay, I'll bite," he said. "What are you doing with yourself these days, Kirsty?"

A middle-aged woman in a cheap cloth coat coughed pointedly behind Kirsty. Kirsty turned and glared at the woman. "I won't be much longer," she said. "Mr Slater and I are old friends. Up until the point where he tried to kill me." She smiled frostily at the woman and then turned back to Slater. "I've written a book," she said. "A novel."

"Really?"

"Really."

"And do you have a publisher?"

She smiled. It wasn't a very nice smile, Slater realized. He picked up the book again and offered it to her, but she still refused to take it from him. "Aren't you going to ask me what it's about? My book?"

Slater sighed and looked at his watch again.

"Come on now, Adrian, you can spare me a minute or two, can't you? After all we've been through."

Slater put the book back on the table, linked the fingers of his hands and looked at her expectantly. "What's your book about, Kirsty?"

"It's an everyday story of boy meets girl, boy screws girl, boy tries to kill girl, girl escapes, boy runs off to New York to kill another girl and write a best-seller."

"It sounds… interesting."

"It is."

"Are you thinking about self-publishing ?"

She shook her head. "Oh no, it's too good for that. One of the big six will take it, I'm sure. It's going to fly off the shelves."

"Well, I wish you all the luck in the world."

"That's nice of you, Adrian." She tapped her lips with the first and second fingers of her right hand. "Silly me, I forgot to tell you about the twist."

"The twist?"

"Well there's got to be a twist, hasn't there." She slipped her hand inside her bag. "If there's no twist, the reader feels cheated. There has to be a twist. And once I've got my twist, then the book will sell itself." Her hand emerged from the bag holding a chrome snub-nosed revolver.

Slater pushed himself back in his seat, his palms face down on the table. "Kirsty, don't do this."

"It has to be done, Adrian. The writer in you knows that." She smiled. "So here's the twist. Girl kills boy. Then writes her own best-seller explaining why she did it and makes a million bucks." She grinned. "And not a vampire or a werewolf in sight."

Slater shook his head. "It's just a story," he said.

"Oh no, Adrian. It's so much more than that." She smiled again. It was the smile of someone who really didn't care about anything.

"Kirsty, please…"

She shook her head sadly and pulled the trigger, shooting him just below the heart. She was still smiling as she pulled the trigger again. And again. And again.

THE END

About the Author

Stephen Leather is one of the UK's most successful thriller writers, an eBook and Sunday Times bestseller and author of the critically acclaimed Dan "Spider' Shepherd series and the Jack Nightingale supernatural detective novels. Before becoming a novelist he was a journalist for more than ten years on newspapers such as The Times, the Daily Mirror, the Glasgow Herald, the Daily Mail and the South China Morning Post in Hong Kong. He is one of the country's most successful eBook authors and his eBooks have topped the Amazon Kindle charts in the UK and the US. The Bookseller magazine named him as one of the 100 most influential people in the UK publishing world and Amazon has identified him as one of their Top 10 UK independent self-publishers. You can visit his website at www.stephenleather.com

Printed in Great Britain
by Amazon